# STINKY & STAN BLAST OFF!

STINKY          STAN

by Annie Auerbach

manga**chapters**™

| | |
|---|---|
| AUTHOR | Annie Auerbach |
| ILLUSTRATOR | Jamar Nicholas |
| DESIGN AND LAYOUT | Erika Terriquez |
| COVER DESIGN | Anne Marie Horne |
| | |
| SENIOR EDITOR | Nicole Monastirsky |
| DIGITAL IMAGING MANAGER | Chris Buford |
| PRE-PRESS SUPERVISOR | Erika Terriquez |
| ART DIRECTOR | Anne Marie Horne |
| PRODUCTION MANAGER | Elisabeth Brizzi |
| MANAGING EDITOR | Vy Nguyen |
| VP OF PRODUCTION | Ron Klamert |
| EDITOR-IN-CHIEF | Rob Tokar |
| PUBLISHER | Mike Kiley |
| PRESIDENT AND C.O.O. | John Parker |
| C.E.O. & CHIEF CREATIVE OFFICER | Stuart Levy |

First TOKYOPOP printing: January 2007

10  9  8  7  6  5  4  3  2  1

Printed in the USA

Library of Congress Cataloging-in-Publication Data

Auerbach, Annie.
  Stinky & Stan Blast Off! / written by Annie Auerbach ; illustrated by Jamar Nicholas.
    p. cm. -- (The Grosse adventures)
"A TOKYOPOP, Inc. Manga Chapter."
  Chapter book, with manga-style illustrations interspersed.
  Summary: The Aliens on Uranus find Stinky & Stan's rocket and note, and decide to head to Earth to retrieve the famous farting brothers and bring them back to their planet, but when the boys realize that the aliens are up to no good they craft a getaway plan to return home.
    ISBN 978-1-59816-050-5 (alk. paper)
    [1. Rockets (Aeronautics)--Fiction. 2. Science--Exhibitions--Fiction. 3. Flatulence--Fiction.  4. Brothers--Fiction. 5. Twins--Fiction. 6. Schools--Fiction. 7. Humorous stories.] I. Jamar Nicholas, ill.
II. Title.
PZ7.A9118Goo 2006                          2006016454
[Fic]--dc22

*For my brothers, Michael and Matt,*
*who have special abilities of their own.*

*—A.A.*

# CONTENTS

## CHAPTER ONE

## ALIEN INVASION!

I bet you didn't know there were aliens on Uranus. Neither did Stinky and Stan. That is until the aliens came looking for *them*.

Stinky and Stan Grosse were not ordinary brothers. They each had an amazing farting ability. Stinky's farts were so smelly that skunks ran for cover when they saw him coming. Stan's farts, on the other hand, were loud and proud—

nearly strong enough to blow a door right off its hinges.

Together, they were the gassiest brothers in the universe! (And I mean the *entire* universe!)

Now the trouble all started when Stinky and Stan were competing in the

Fourth Grade Astronomy Fair at school. After many failed attempts, they finally got their rocket to launch.

It launched all right . . . right into space! Well, if you want to be technical, it landed on Uranus—and was discovered by aliens!

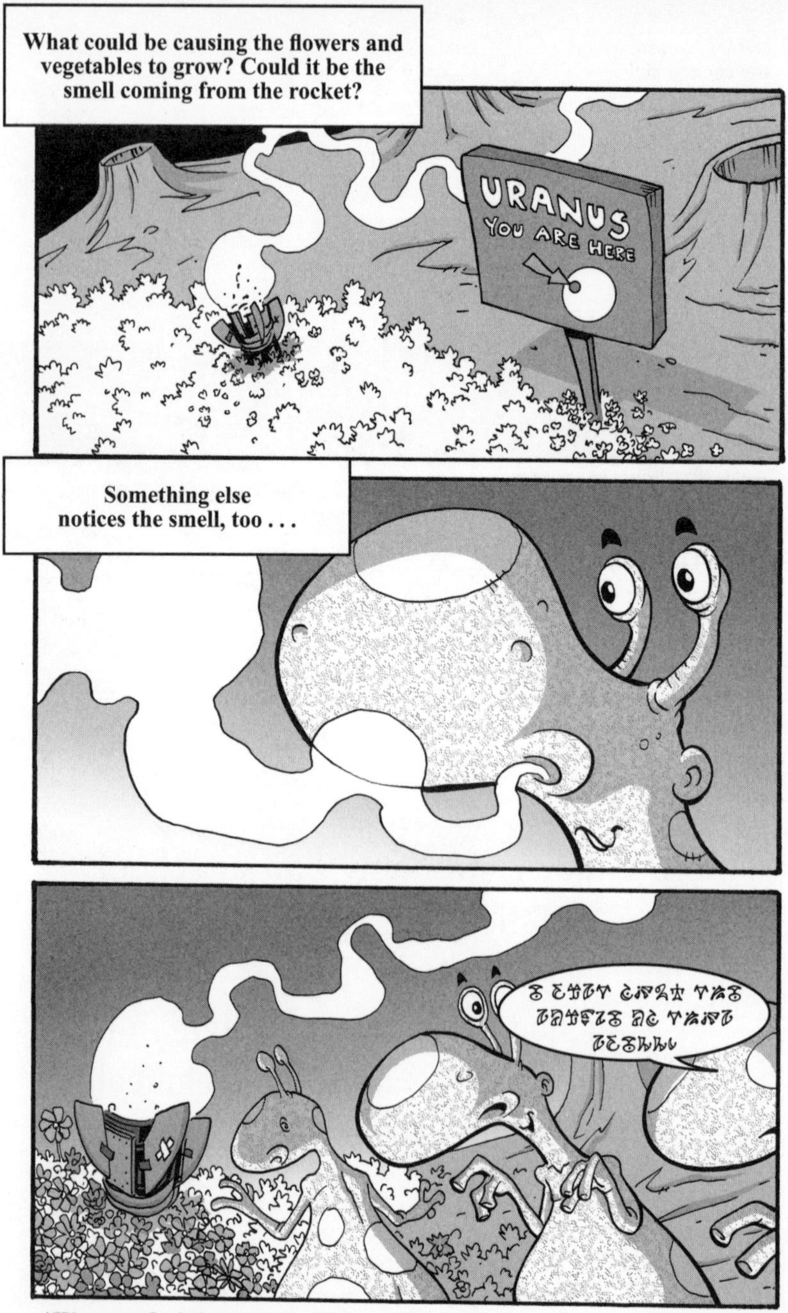
What could be causing the flowers and vegetables to grow? Could it be the smell coming from the rocket?
URANUS
YOU ARE HERE
Something else notices the smell, too . . .

*We must find the source of this smell!

*The smell is coming from the rocket, sir!

*But we must find the original source!

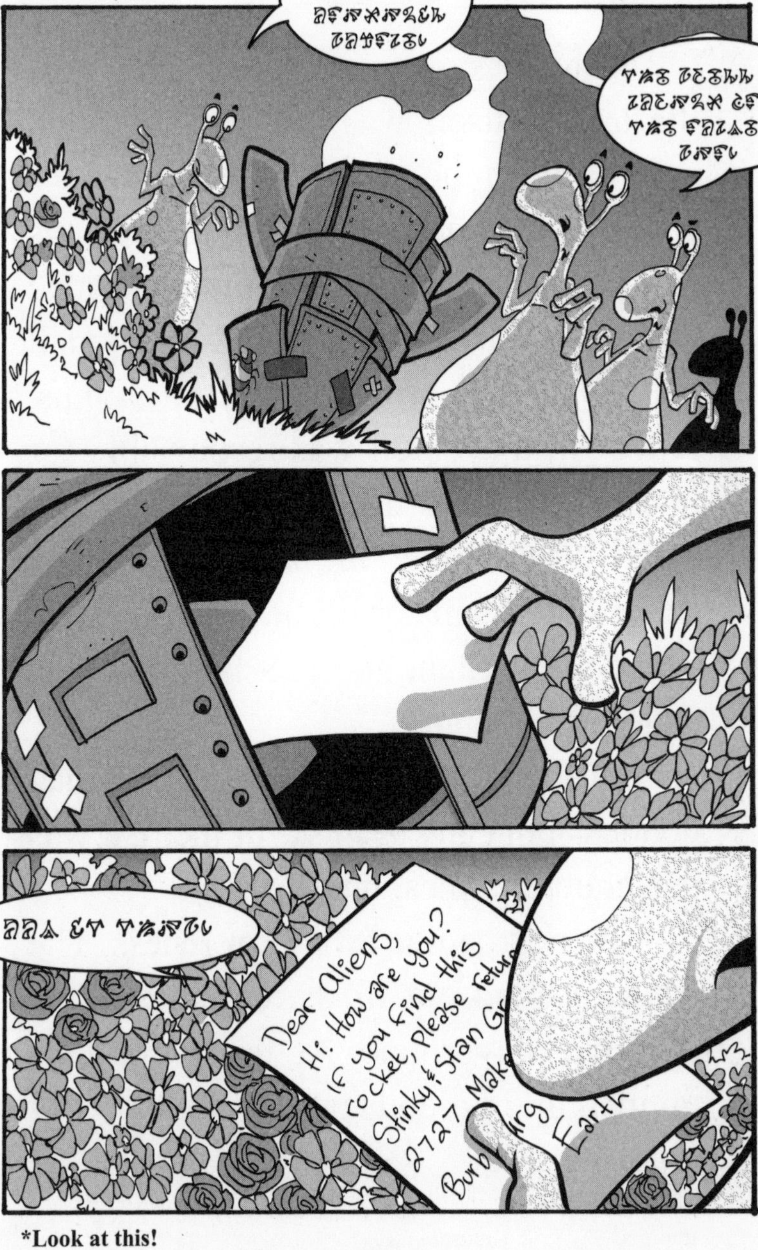
Dear Aliens,
Hi. How are you?
If you find this
rocket, please
Stinky & Stan
2727
Earth

*Look at this!

What was even more exciting than the launch itself was the unusual smell coming from the rocket.

After the aliens read the note the boys had put in the rocket, the aliens decided that they *had* to find out how the smell was made and bring it back to Uranus. After all, this smell was responsible for making Uranus's flowers bloom!

With the note in hand, the aliens immediately left for Earth. It was time to find Stinky, Stan, and this faraway land called "Burbsburg."

Back on Earth, Stinky and Stan had no idea about any of this. For them, it was just another typical day at school . . .

The bell had just rung for recess. The students filed out of the classroom and onto the playground. As usual, the kids divided up into their own groups:

There was Penelope Parsnippity and her wanna-bes, Tiffanie and Steffanie. The three girls were sitting on some benches debating whether you could wear a brown belt with a black skirt.

Stinky and Stan sat on the other side of the playground with their friend, Eugene Clunkenheimer, and the foreign exchange student who no one could understand, Grñpæk Yvlåöqçkn. The collective brainpower sitting there was amazing, but to the outside world, it looked like geek central. Eugene had brought his Transalienator to school. It was a device he and Grñpæk, or "G" as they called him, had developed for the Astronomy Fair. Eugene had hoped to talk to aliens with it someday, but it didn't work right. It kept translating things incorrectly. Until aliens actually showed up, the boys used it to *try* to translate what Grñpæk said.

"How does this thing work again?" asked Stan.

Eugene was more than happy to explain. "G talks into the mouthpiece here and the machine translates it. I've been tinkering with it, and I think I've got it working right," said Eugene, with a loud sneeze. Eugene was allergic to just about everything under the sun. After he blew his nose (which sounded like a trumpet), he handed the mouthpiece of the Transalienator to Grñpæk.

Grñpæk swallowed the bite of apple he was chewing. Then he took the mouthpiece and spoke into it: "Z ptttqww xbxrq mqrtiiip."

The machine translated that to: "I like apples up my nose."

Everyone burst out into laughter. Everyone except Eugene.

Stan reassured him. "Hey, at least now it's getting more words *right* than wrong!"

Eugene was about to respond when a shadow fell across the group. Was it a cloud? Was it a plane? Was it a monster?

Well, almost . . . it was Penelope and her friends.

"Poor Eugene. Still waiting for aliens to show up at your front door?" Penelope said to him, looking at the Transalienator.

Stinky jumped in to defend Eugene. "Poor Penelope. Still searching for intelligent life forms to become your friends?"

Penelope narrowed her eyes. Stinky Grosse was one of her least favorite people.

"At least *my* friends aren't total goobers. Come on, let's go," Penelope said.

"Yeah, like, let's get out of here," replied Tiffanie.

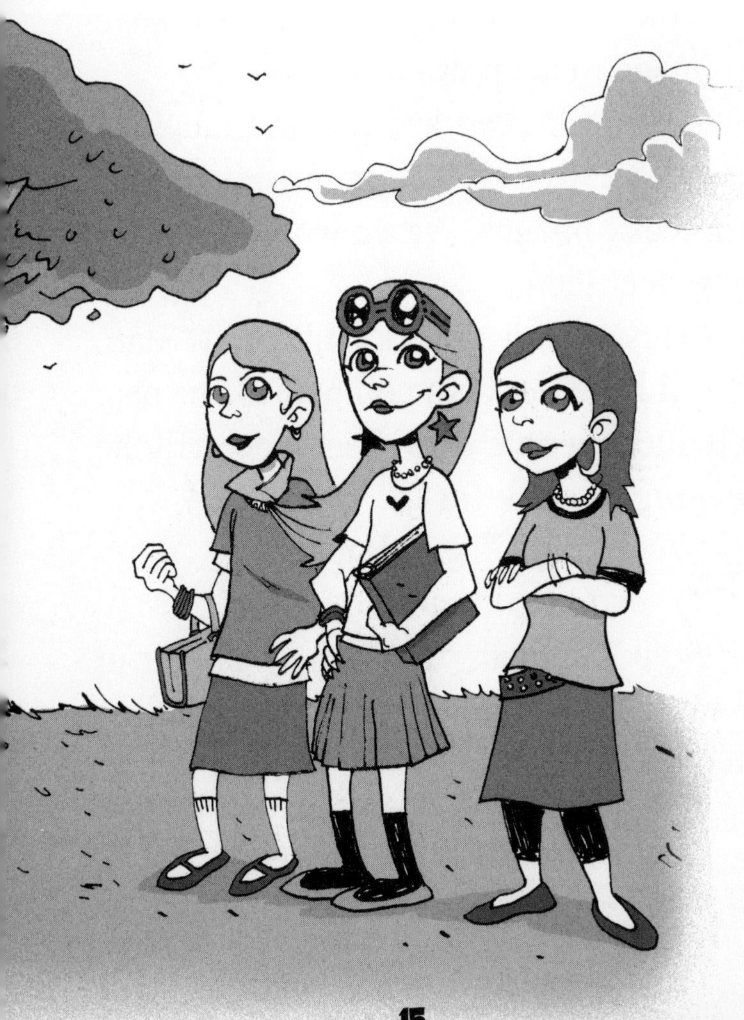

"Totally," was all Steffanie could think of to add.

"We don't want to be seen next to you, either!" Stan yelled back. Then to the others he added, "After all, we have an image to keep up."

Eugene looked at Stan and laughed. "Yeah, we wouldn't want anyone to ruin our geeky images. We've worked so hard to perfect them."

"Hey, don't knock it," said Stan. "We'll have our own companies one day, and then people like Penelope will be *begging* to work for us."

"Yeah, right," said Eugene.

"Ymvddqqp!" said Grñpæk.

Stinky sighed. "I'll hope we'll fit in somewhere, someday," he said under his breath.

## CHAPTER TWO

### THE NOSE KNOWS

Perhaps life wasn't particularly *easy* for the brothers, but it sure was fun! Their most favorite thing to do was to go exploring. Whether it was uncovering forgotten treasures in the neighborhood scrap yard or creating an imaginative world right in their own backyard, those two were always up to something.

At the moment, the brothers were exploring the moon . . .

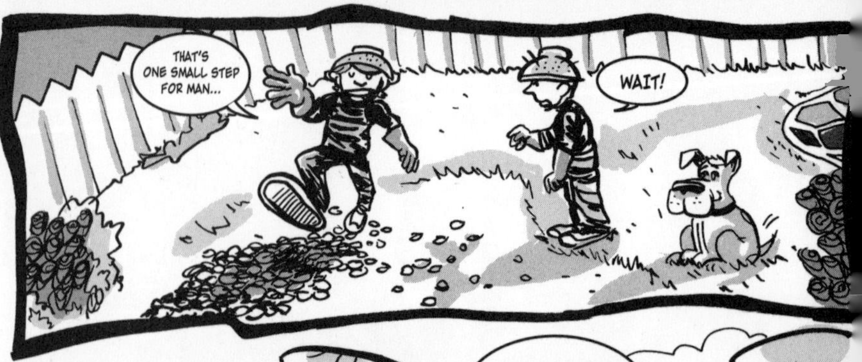
THAT'S ONE SMALL STEP FOR MAN...
WAIT!

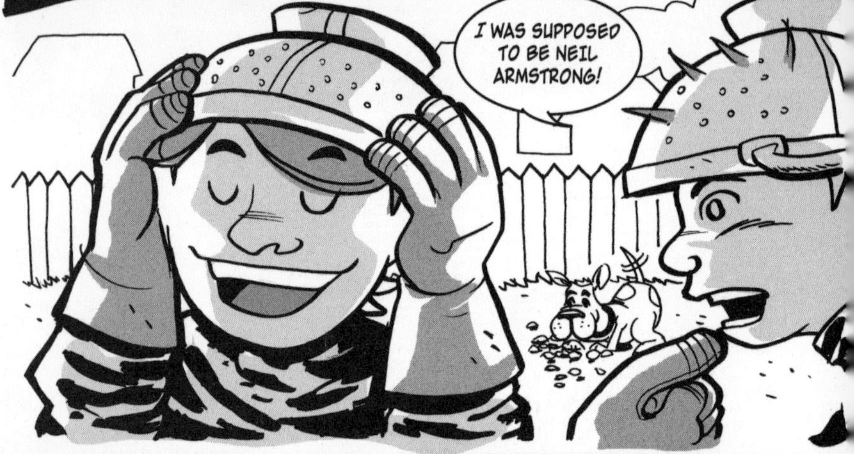
I WAS SUPPOSED TO BE NEIL ARMSTRONG!

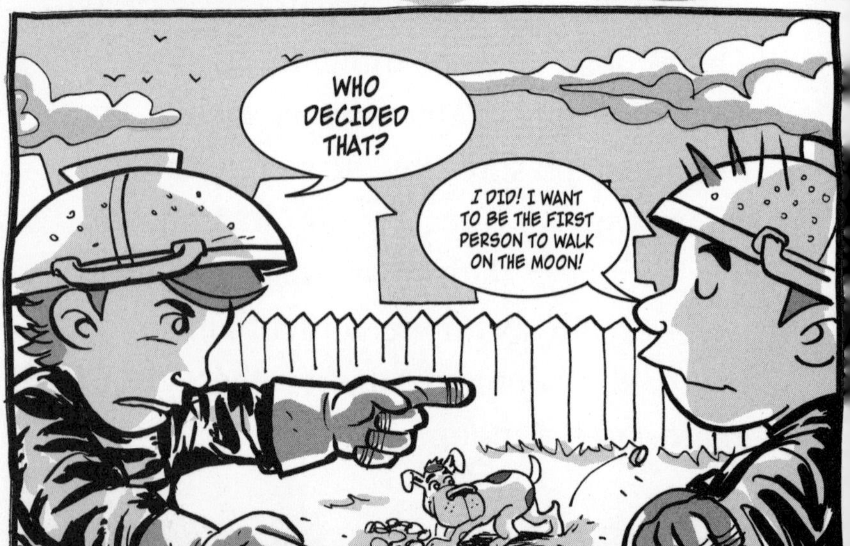
WHO DECIDED THAT?
I DID! I WANT TO BE THE FIRST PERSON TO WALK ON THE MOON!

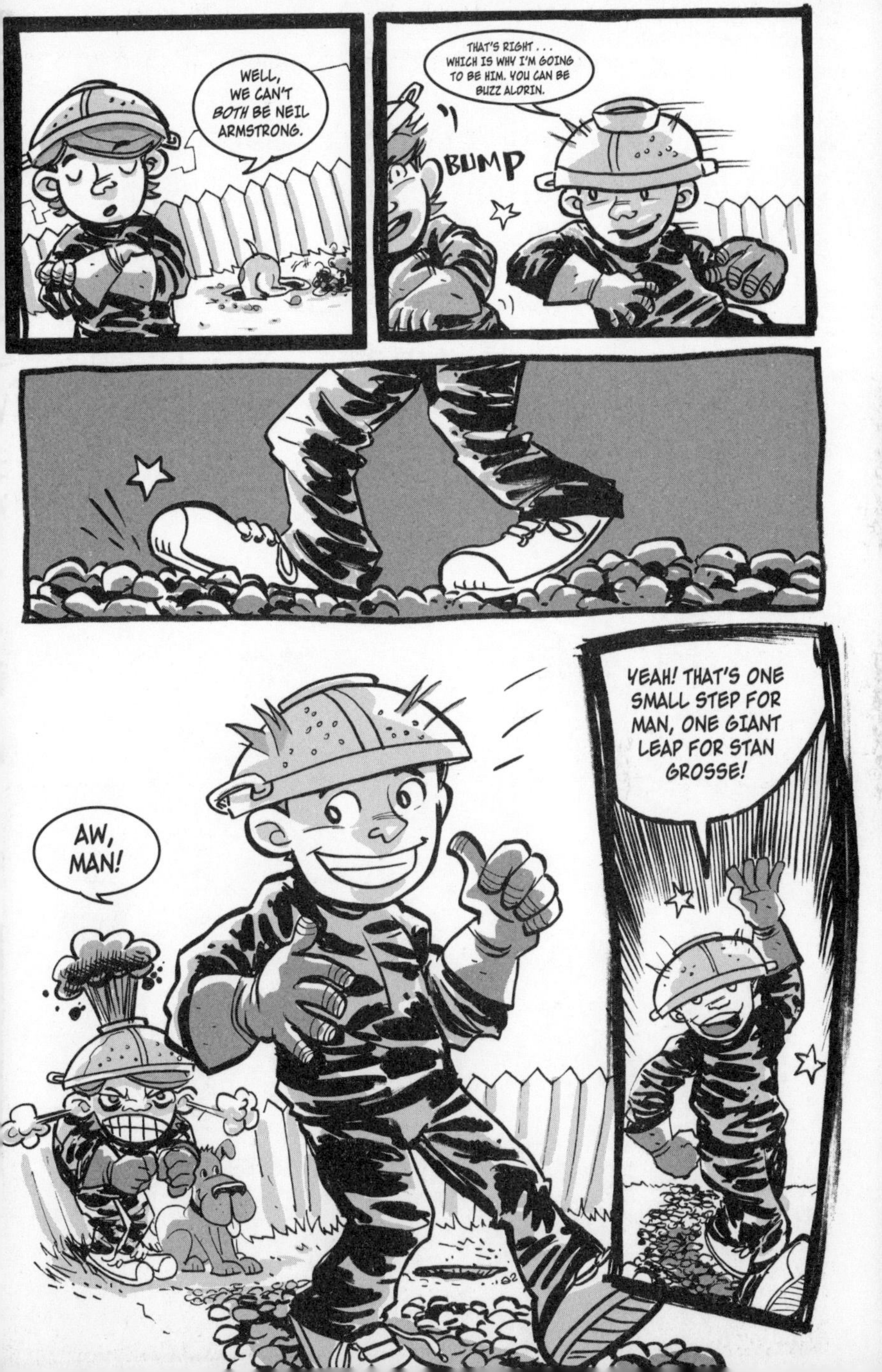
WELL, WE CAN'T *BOTH* BE NEIL ARMSTRONG.
THAT'S RIGHT . . . WHICH IS WHY I'M GOING TO BE HIM. YOU CAN BE BUZZ ALDRIN.
BUMP
AW, MAN!
YEAH! THAT'S ONE SMALL STEP FOR MAN, ONE GIANT LEAP FOR STAN GROSSE!

Meanwhile, in *actual* outer space, two aliens from Uranus were bound for Earth. The spaceship's pilot was a heavy-set alien named Nerk. The other, a thinner and nervous alien, was named Fring. They had a very important job to do: find Stinky and Stan Grosse.

Fring

Nerk

Unfortunately, their spaceship's computer-guided navigation system was on the blink. Nerk and Fring had tried to buy an Earth map at the M.O.U.O.P. store (Maps of Uranus & Other Planets), but they were all sold out. It was tourist season, after all.

The alien ship soared past Saturn's rings and made a left turn at Jupiter's fiery red spot. Once they passed Mars, they could see Earth in the distance. Fring jumped with excitement.

"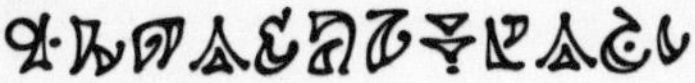!" he cried.

Nerk told Fring to hold on as he turned the ship and zoomed toward Earth.

Once in Earth's atmosphere, the aliens had a little trouble locating Burbsburg. Fring wanted to stop and ask for directions, but Nerk refused. Hours and hours passed, but all they saw below them were enormous oceans.

Eventually, they began to fly over houses and baseball fields. They started flying lower, and Nerk spotted a sign that read:

Burbsburg — 3 miles
Muttontown — 30 miles
Lummoxville — 50 miles

"ᎥᎦᏋⲗⲗⲗᎥᎯᏠᎥᏗᏋᎥ," they said to each other in their alien language. They were close!

Before long, the aliens were in Burbs-burg and searching for Stinky and Stan's exact address: 2727 Makenmegag Road.

A few wrong turns and barking dogs later, the aliens finally found the correct address. Nerk silently landed their spaceship on the Grosse family's roof.

The hatch from the spaceship opened, and Nerk and Fring slowly waddled out. Their eyes nervously darted around; they had to be on guard at all times. After all, who knew what sort of weird creatures they might find there?!

Nerk carefully walked to the edge of the roof and looked down into Stinky and Stan's backyard. They saw two boys in what looked like some kind of armor.

"ﾌﾞﾒﾝﾃﾞﾂ," he said and motioned to Fring.

Fring walked over to Nerk and cried out "ﾂﾞﾌﾞﾃﾞ!" in excitement.

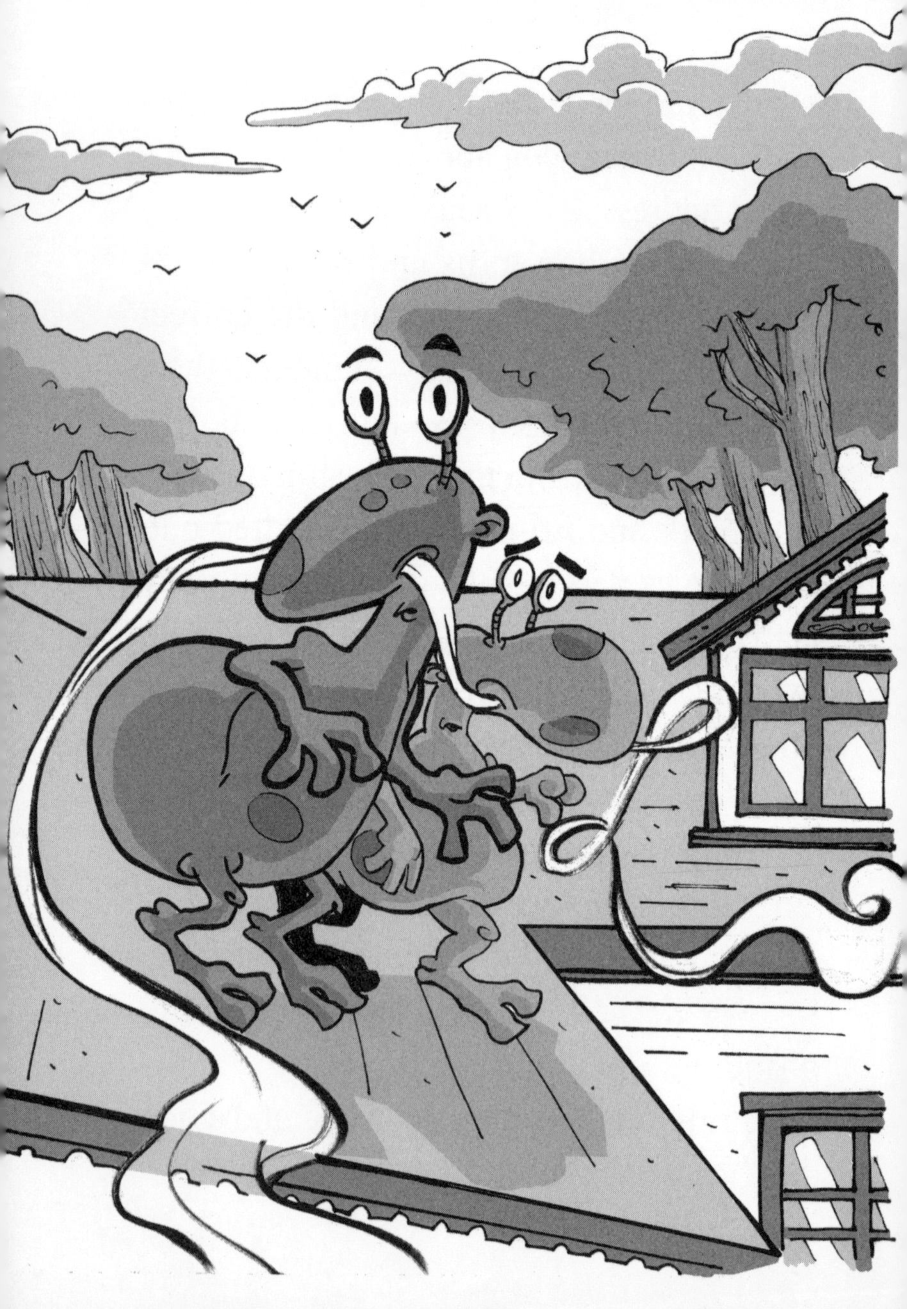

*They even look like royalty,* thought Fring, referring to the boys' tin foil spacesuits.

But Nerk was worried. What if those boys weren't Stinky and Stan Grosse?

A rotten smell wafted up from below. Suddenly Nerk and Fring had no doubt that they were most definitely at the right house.

The aliens jumped off the roof. They landed on their big cushiony butts, so the fall didn't hurt. In fact, Fring bounced back up onto the roof! They certainly weren't used to this strange planet.

Nerk and Fring approached Stinky and Stan, who were still pretending to walk on the moon. The aliens immediately bowed down to the boys because they believed Stinky and Stan were responsible for making Uranus's vegetables and flowers grow. The aliens came in peace . . . unlike Columbus the dog, who wouldn't stop barking.

"Whoa!" exclaimed Stan.

"What in the world?!" exclaimed Stinky.

"Am I dreaming?" asked Stan, rubbing his eyes.

"That's impossible," answered Stinky. "How could we both be having the same dream?"

"But there are ALIENS in our backyard!" cried Stan.

"Shhh!" said Stinky. *"I* know! But *everyone* doesn't have to know that!"

Stinky gestured for Stan and the aliens to follow him to hide behind a nearby tree.

The aliens eagerly followed and once there, Nerk said, "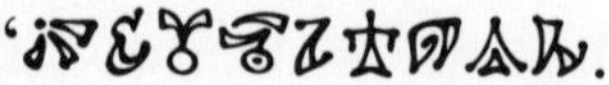."

Stinky and Stan exchanged puzzled looks.

Then Stan spoke slowly. "Welcome to Earth. Where are you from?"

This time, it was Nerk and Fring who exchanged puzzled looks.

Fring said, "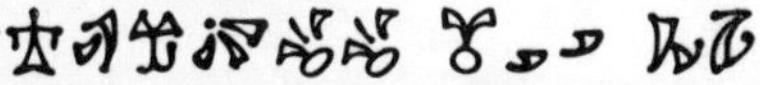."

Stinky thought he heard the word "pickle" in there, but wouldn't swear to it. Stan was secretly wishing he had watched *Star Wars* a few hundred times more.

Then all of a sudden, nothing else mattered except the new danger on the horizon: Mom!

"Stinky! Stan!" called Mrs. Grosse.

Oh, no! How would the boys be able to explain the aliens, or the fact that their homework wasn't done yet?

## CHAPTER THREE

## DO YOU SEE WHAT I SEE?

"Stinky! Stan?!" Mrs. Grosse called again. "Can you give me a hand with the groceries?"

The boys had to think quickly.

"Uh . . . sure! Be right there!" Stinky yelled back. He turned to Stan and whispered, "Let's take the aliens to our room, then I'll go help Mom."

The aliens were puzzled by what was happening as the boys pushed them inside.

But the aliens couldn't move very fast because their big butts wouldn't let them fit through the doorways!

"They're stuck!" whispered Stan. "They should have taken it easy on that alien pizza!"

"Sideways! Sideways!" said Stinky. "Turn them sideways!"

After walking sideways to get through the doorways, the aliens managed to make it safely to Stinky and Stan's bedroom.

"Whew! That was a close call," Stan said, as he quickly shut the door.

"No time to rest," said Stinky. "I've got to go help Mom."

"Okay. I'll go call Eugene and tell him to bring over his Transalienator," suggested Stan. "Maybe then we'll be able to understand the aliens."

"Good thinking," said Stinky. "I'll meet you back here."

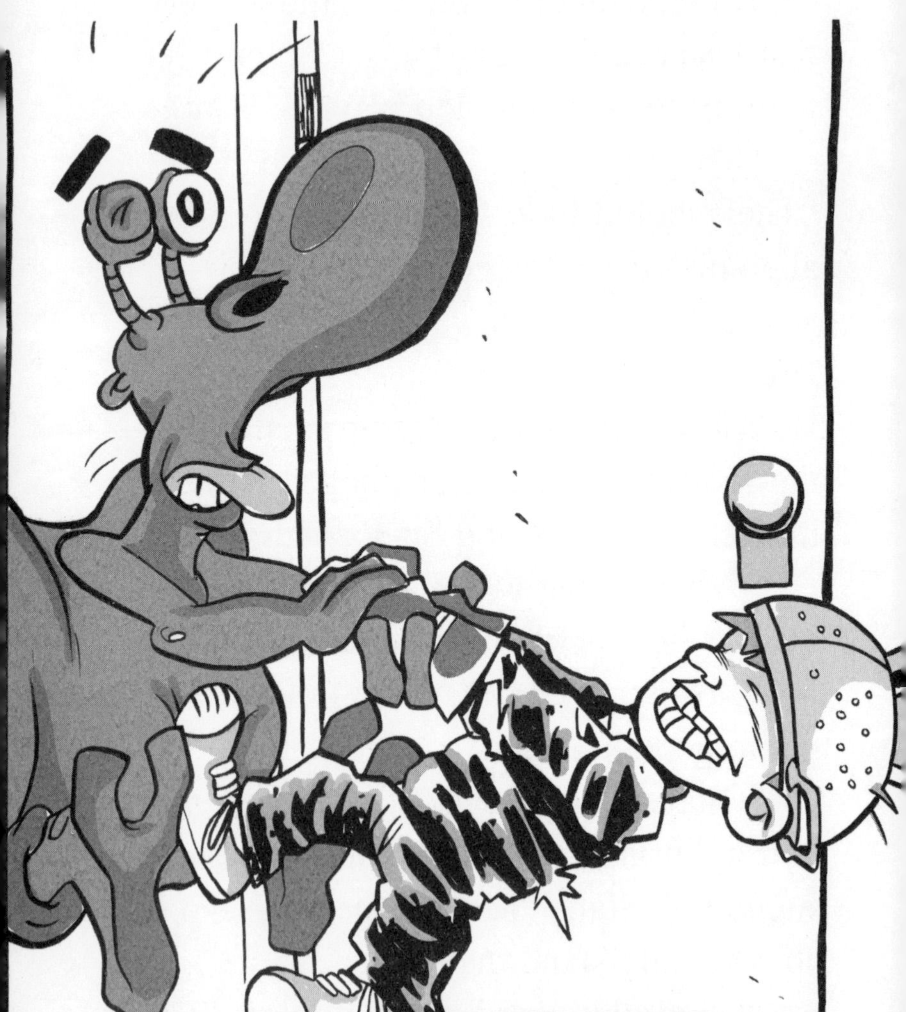

Then the boys motioned to the confused aliens to stay put.

"Think they understood?" Stinky asked.

"I hope so!" said Stan as they left.

Inside the boys' room, Nerk and Fring looked at one another, confused. Then they looked around. There were tons of books, posters, and clothes lying everywhere.

Suddenly, Nerk yelped. Fring turned around to see what was wrong.

Then he saw them, too . . . an entire toy box full of shrunken aliens!

Of course, you and I both know these were just toys. But the aliens didn't know that. To them, this was danger with a capital D! (Or whatever it was in their language!)

Nerk carefully picked up one of the toy aliens. His eyes widened when he moved the alien's arm and it locked in place!

“[illegible]!!!” screamed Nerk and Fring. (No need to translate that for you.)

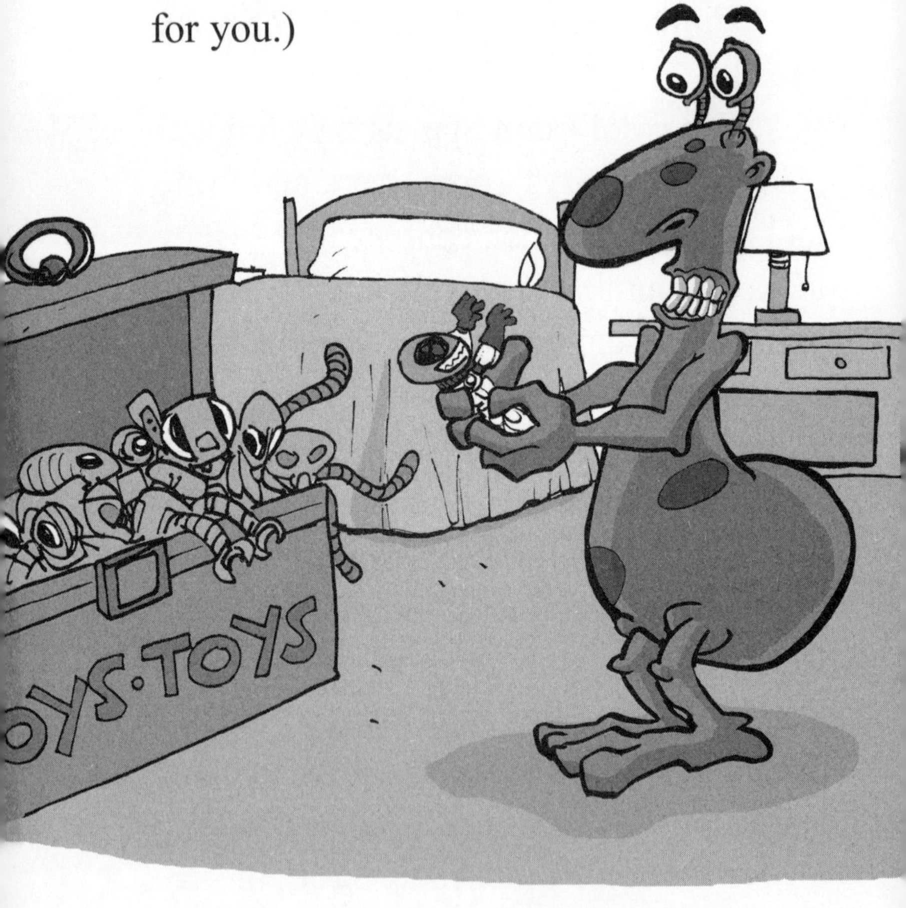
OYS·TOYS

Nerk and Fring decided right then and there that Stinky and Stan were very dangerous. But the aliens still needed them so that Uranus's vegetation would continue to flower and grow. Nerk and Fring realized they'd better be very careful, or they might end up tiny and frozen, too!

But there was another threat lurking, and this one was right down the hall . . .

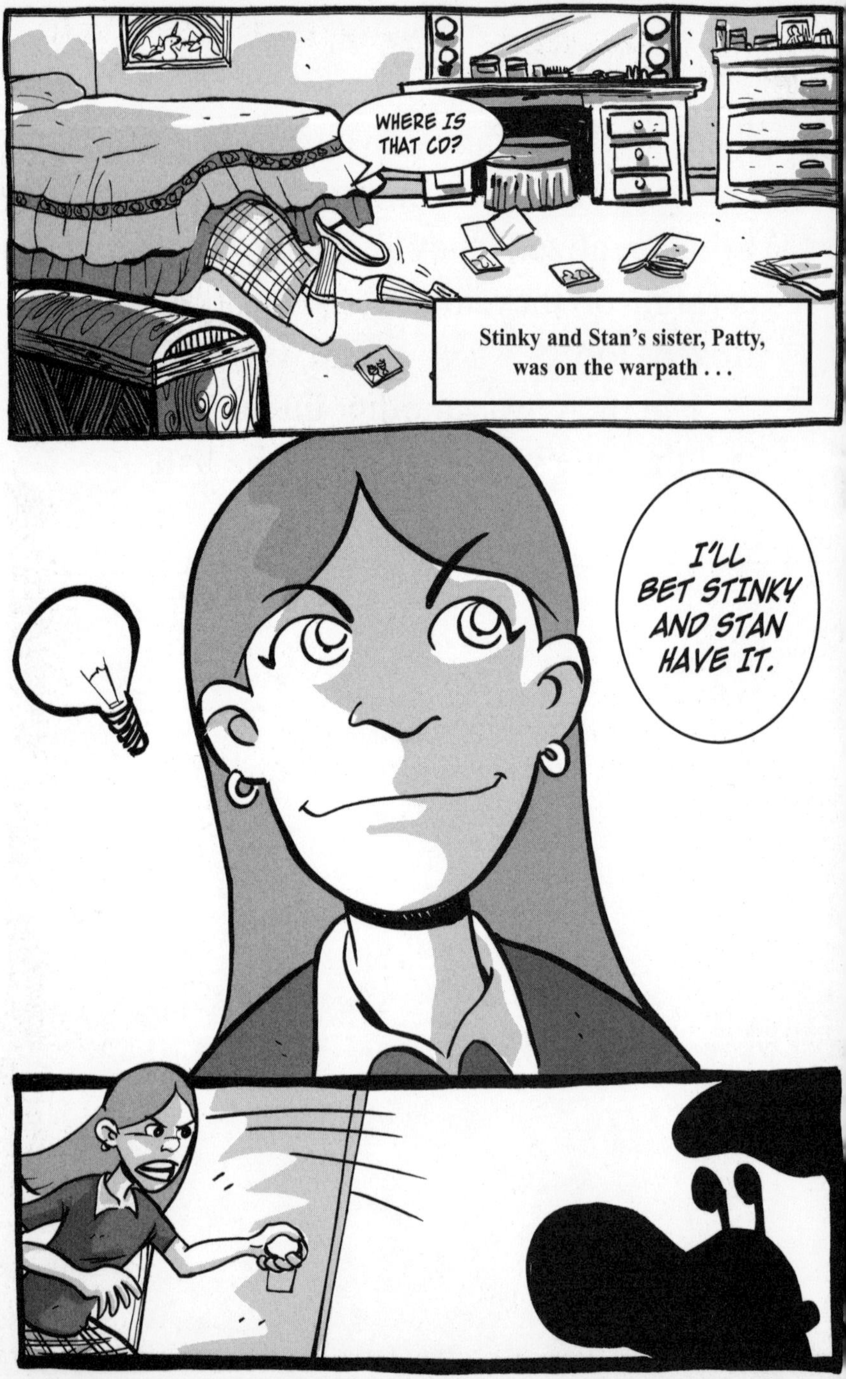
WHERE IS THAT CD?
Stinky and Stan's sister, Patty, was on the warpath . . .
I'LL BET STINKY AND STAN HAVE IT.

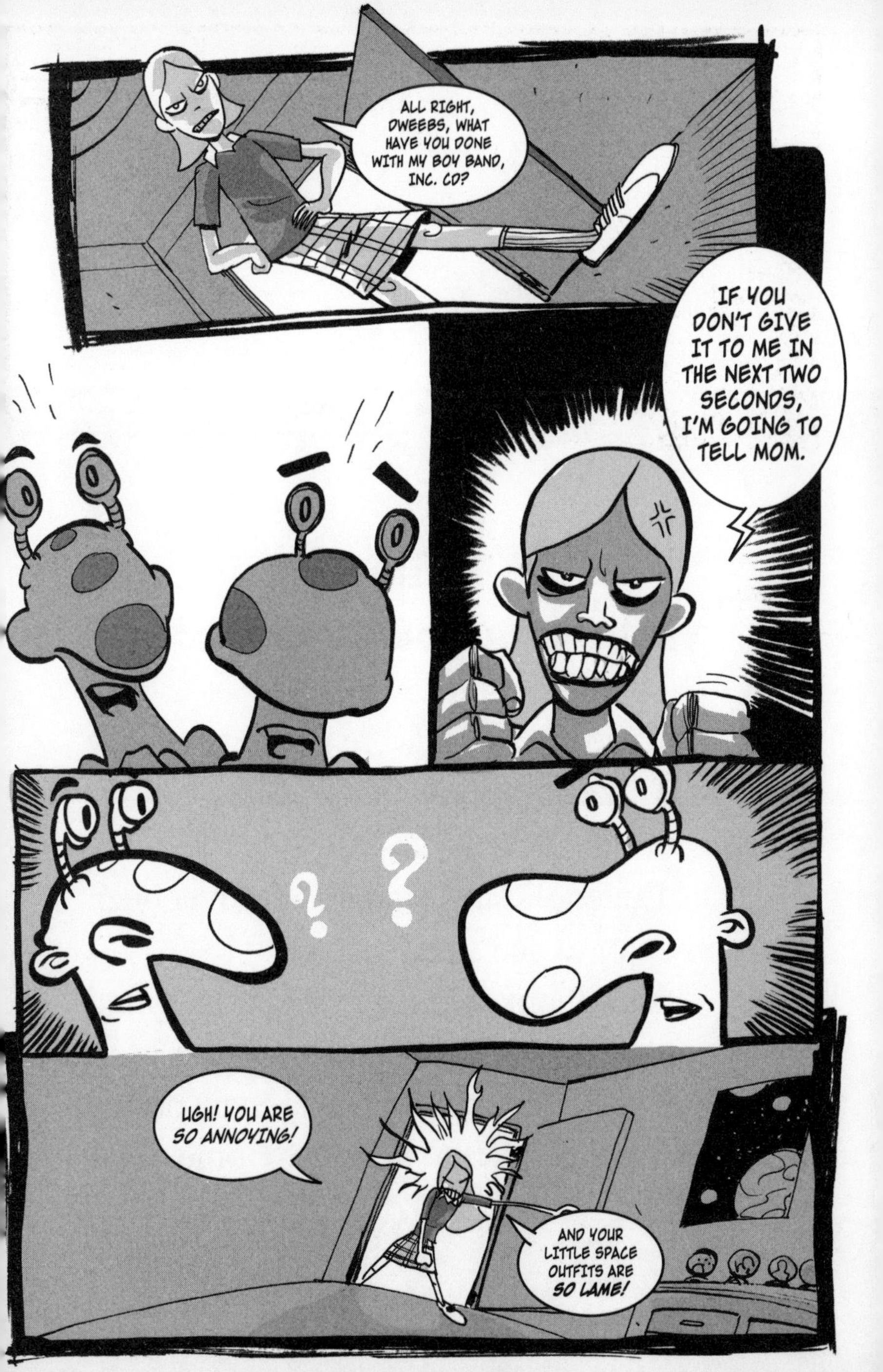
ALL RIGHT, DWEEBS, WHAT HAVE YOU DONE WITH MY BOY BAND, INC. CD?
IF YOU DON'T GIVE IT TO ME IN THE NEXT TWO SECONDS, I'M GOING TO TELL MOM.
?
?
UGH! YOU ARE SO ANNOYING!
AND YOUR LITTLE SPACE OUTFITS ARE SO LAME!

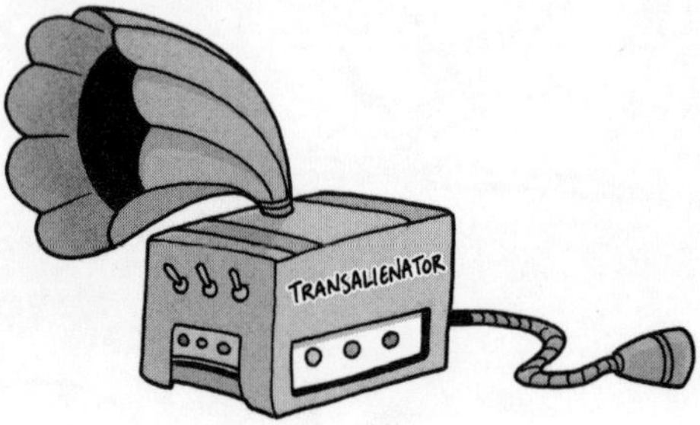
TRANSALIENATOR

## CHAPTER FOUR

# TRANSALIENATOR TO THE RESCUE

While the aliens were getting to know Patty, the doorbell rang. Stan ran to answer it.

"Eugene!" said Stan. "I've never been so happy to see you."

"Uh, thanks . . . I think," replied Eugene.

Without missing a beat, Stan pulled Eugene inside the house. "Come with me," he said.

By the time Stan and Eugene walked to the bedroom, Stinky was already at the door, keeping guard.

"Oh, good! You're here," Stinky whispered to Eugene. "And you brought the Transalienator?"

"Yes," replied Eugene. "But what do you need it for? And why are we whispering?"

"You'll see," replied Stinky.

Stan made sure the coast was clear and then nodded to his brother. Stinky opened the door and the three boys hustled inside.

Eugene turned around, saw Nerk and Fring, and immediately passed out.

"Eugene!" cried Stan. "What's wrong? This is what you've been waiting for your whole life!"

But Eugene was down, and he wasn't getting up any time soon.

"Well," said Stan, "if Eugene can't use the Transalienator on the aliens, then I guess *we'd* better try to."

Luckily, the boys remembered how to work the device. Stan took the mouthpiece and said "h-e-l-l-o" into it.

The aliens heard "ठ☆ऽ刁Ꮭᵛ☺ᗷ" and wondered where the sound was coming from. They looked around the room for other aliens, and then they stared at the tiny, frozen aliens they were holding in their hands.

Stan started to hand the mouthpiece to Fring, who promptly put it in his mouth.

"No!" cried Stan. "Don't *eat* it, *talk into* it."

Nerk seemed to understand and made some noise into the Transalienator:

Out came, "I am Nerk and this is Fring. We are from Uranus."

Immediately, Stinky and Stan busted up in laughter. (Let's face it, no matter who you are or where you're from, Uranus is a funny word.)

When Stinky stopped laughing, he introduced himself and his brother. "We are Earthlings," Stinky explained.

Stan started to laugh again.

CRUNCH

"What's so funny?" Stinky asked him.

"Well, if we're *Earthlings,* then the aliens must be *Uranusings! Uranus-sings!* Get it?" Stan explained, and they exploded in laughter again.

The Uranusings wondered why the boys were laughing.

"Maybe it's a weird Earthling ritual," Fring whispered to Nerk in their language. Then Nerk grabbed the mouthpiece, made some noise, and the Transalienator spit out: "We found a goat."

"A goat?" asked Stan, confused.

What it meant to say was "note," but the Transalienator was not yet in tip-top operating form.

Nerk grabbed the note that had been inside the rocket. Suddenly Stinky and Stan's eyes widened.

"Our note! You found our note! Our rocket went to Uranus!" they cheered.

Then Stinky composed himself and said, "Shhh! We'd better keep it down or Mom will hear us."

"Or worse: Patty!" whispered Stan.

Nerk then told Stinky and Stan about what happened to the rocket when it crashed on Uranus.

"We believe you two have special powers that make our flowers and vegetables grow," the device translated for Nerk. "Please come to our planet as honored guests. You will be treated like kings." He and Fring bowed.

Stinky and Stan didn't know what to say. They went over to a corner of their room to talk it over.

Stan was gung-ho, but Stinky wasn't so sure.

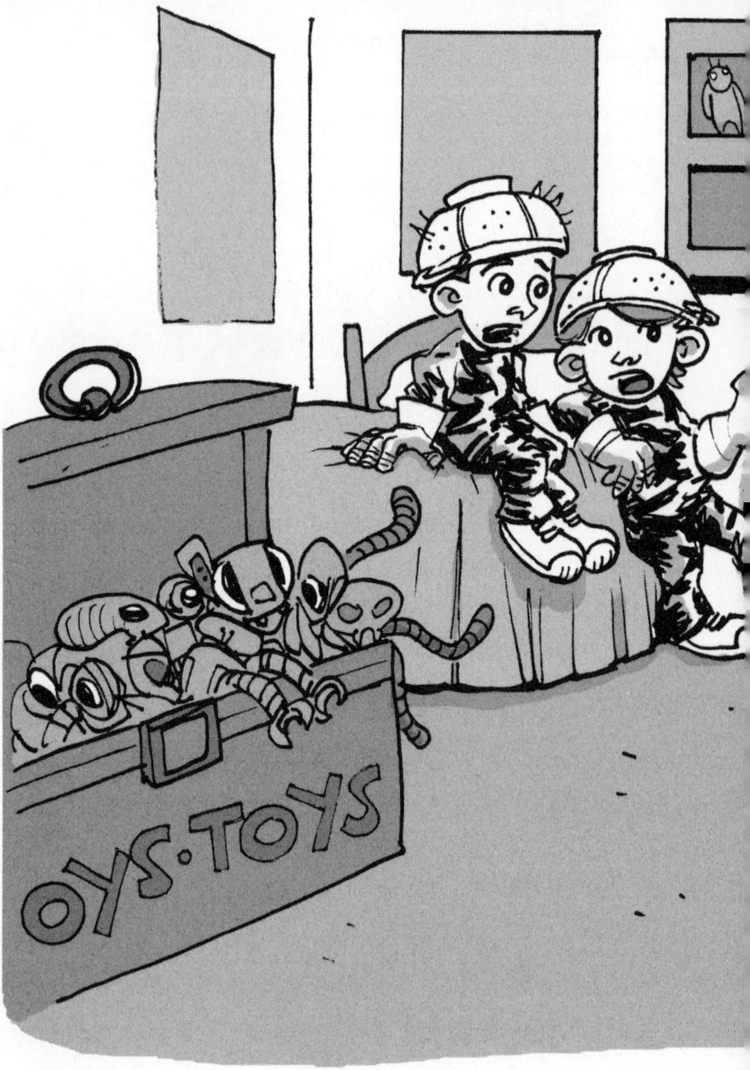
OYS·TOYS

"When else will we possibly have the chance to be treated like royalty?" Stan said excitedly. "I think we should go!"

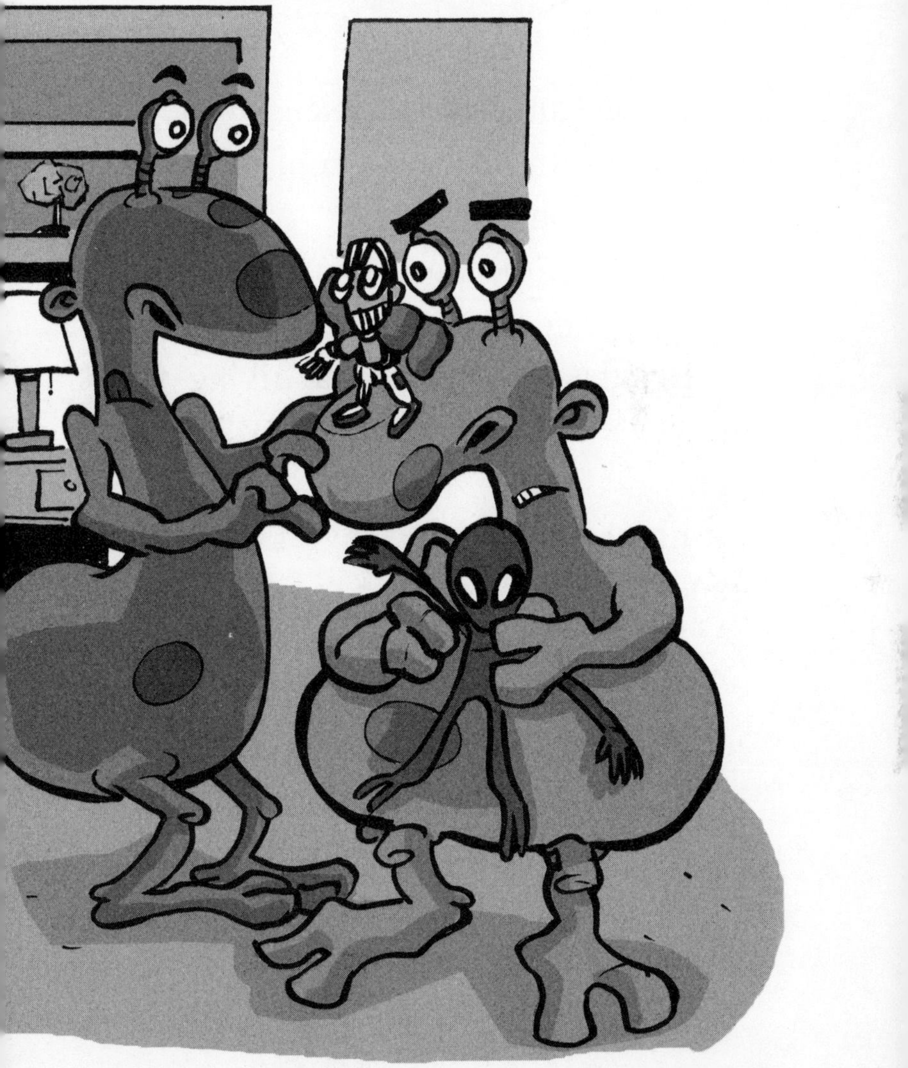

Stinky admitted that it was a tempting offer but he still was unsure. “We don’t know these aliens. What if they’re dangerous?”

Stan gestured to the aliens. "They're playing with action figures. How dangerous could they be?"

Suddenly, the boys could hear Patty yelling from down the hall.

"Besides, we're used to living with aliens . . . just look at Patty," added Stan.

Stinky laughed. "Okay! Let's go to Uranus!"

## CHAPTER FIVE

# A FEAST FIT FOR A KING (OR TWO)

"Wow!" said Stinky as the boys left the spaceship and stepped foot on Uranus.

"Awesome!" said Stan.

All around them was a bustling city. There were oddly shaped skyscrapers, tons of spaceships lining the 405 Flyway, all sorts of restaurants, and even movie theaters. Everywhere the boys looked, there were Uranusings hurrying about.

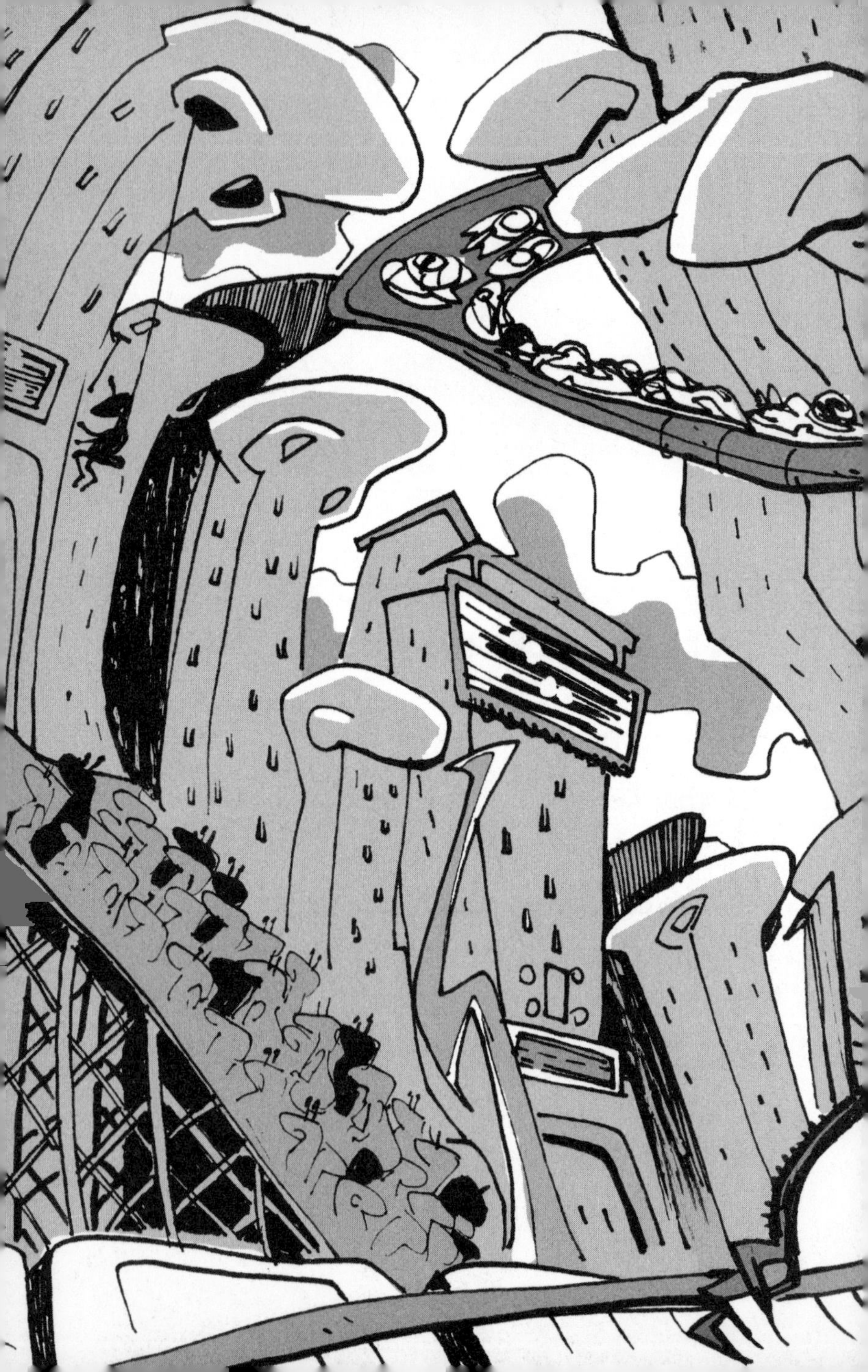

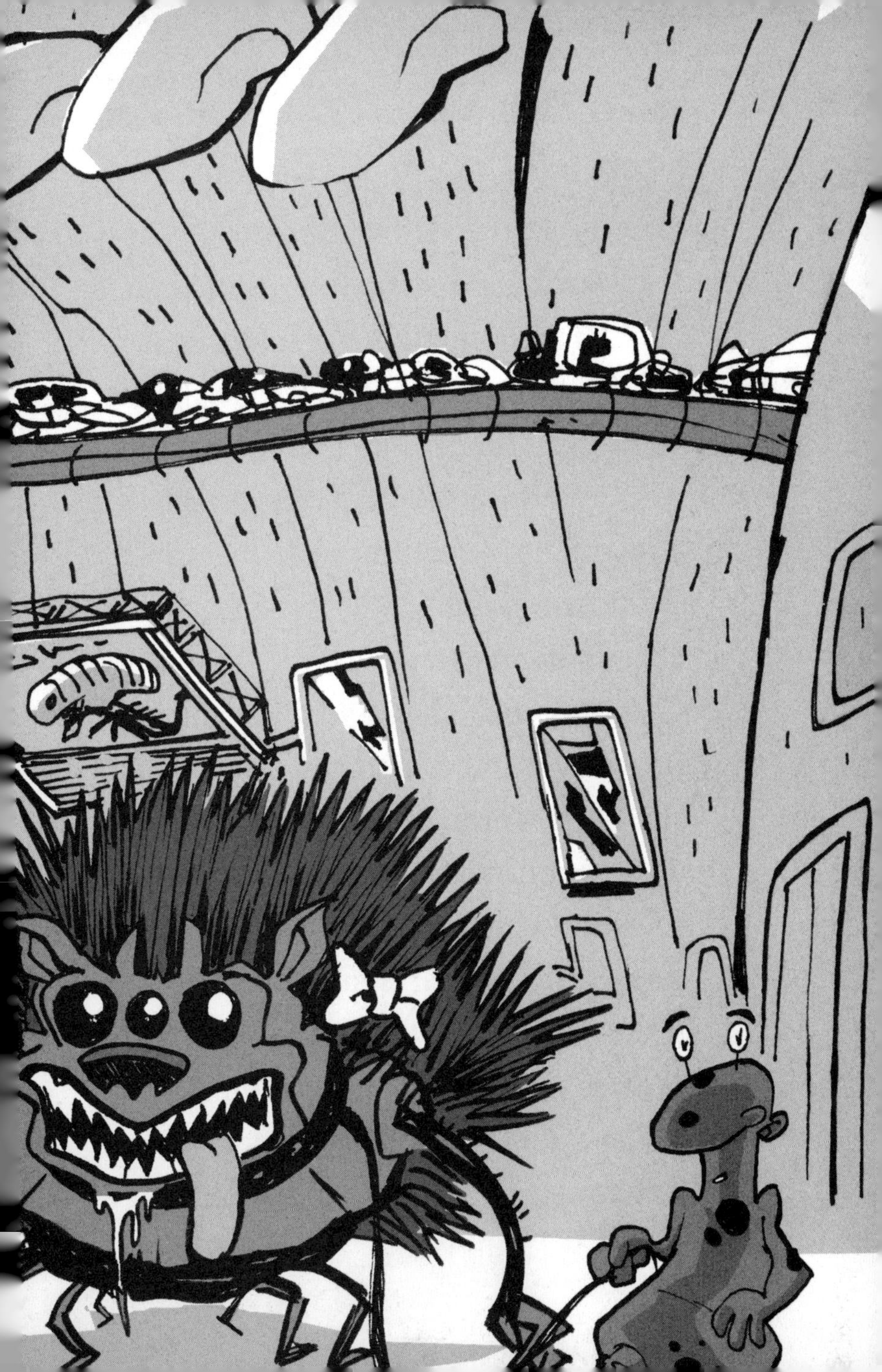

"Whoa!" cried Stan suddenly. He quickly took the Transalienator out of his backpack and turned it on. "What is that?" He pointed to a huge, scary-looking creature being led on a leash by a Uranusing. It looked like giant porcupine with three eyes and sharp fangs. But its most frightening feature were the spikes up and down its back.

"That's a *snufflewoowoo,*" translated Nerk. "They are the sweetest animals and are very popular as pets."

The boys weren't convinced. "I think I'll stick to animals that are smaller than me," Stinky whispered to Stan.

"Me, too!" agreed Stan.

In the distance, Stinky and Stan saw Uranusings propelling up into the sky.

"What's going on?" Stinky asked Nerk, pointing to the Uranusings in the air.

"Ah! The Gas Geysers!" Nerk said. "Come, I'll show you."

A short walk later, they arrived at the Gas Geysers. Stinky and Stan watched in amazement as Uranusings sat in the middle of different geysers and then gas would shoot them all up in the air. There were different geysers that sent them in

*Whoa!

different directions, depending on where they wanted to go.

Nerk explained that since Uranus is such a gassy planet, the residents are able to use its unique gas geysers for transportation.

"That's pretty smart!" said Stan.

"But once the gas shoots them in the air, how do they get down?" Stinky asked.

Nerk smiled and just patted his butt.

"A-ha!" Stinky and Stan said together.

"Now, come," Nerk said into the Transalienator. "Allow me to escort you to the palace for a great feast in your honor."

"A palace? Cool!" said Stinky.

"A feast? Cool!" said Stan. "This is getting better and better by the minute."

Now, this was no ordinary, run-of-the-mill feast. After all, the boys *were* on another planet.

As they entered a large hall, all the Uranusings in the room bowed. Stinky and Stan were led to a magnificent, long table. The chairs they were seated in felt enormous because the boys didn't have large butts.

All along the table there were serving plates full of alien food—creepy-crawly things, slimy-grimy drinks, and bowls that bubbled and burped.

Stinky began to feel a little queasy. Stan suddenly didn't feel that hungry.

"Wow! Is this food or a science experiment?" Stinky whispered out of the side of his mouth.

Just then, a short, stocky Uranusing came by and dished the disgusting delicacies onto the boys' plates.

Stinky and Stan tried not to gag. Even worse, everyone was staring at them.

"Why are they staring at us?" Stan whispered.

"I'm not sure," Stinky whispered back. "Maybe they're waiting for us to begin eating first?"

"But my food is moving!" said Stan.

Sure enough, it was moving. In fact, if Stan didn't hurry, his food was going to scurry away!

The boys knew they had no choice. They didn't want to offend their hosts. There was no silverware, so with his hand, Stan grabbed the creepy-crawly piece of food that was slithering away. Stinky grabbed some food, too. They both tried to smile.

"On the count of three," Stan whispered to Stinky. "One, two, three!"

The boys put the squirming food in their mouths. It took all their might just to swallow it.

A great cheer rose up from the Uranusings. Then they all begin to eat. They crammed the creepy-crawly food into their mouths and guzzled the slimy-grimy drinks.

"At least they're not paying attention to us anymore," Stinky whispered to Stan.

Stan hardly heard his brother. He was too engrossed in watching a piece of alien food crawl down the side of a plate, turn around, and then eat the plate itself!

The alien food was slinking away when it got caught and eaten by a nearby Uranusing. The Uranusing then gave a loud belch and spit out the plate.

"Did you see that?" Stan said to his brother.

"How could I miss it?" Stinky answered, holding his nose. That was one stinky burp!

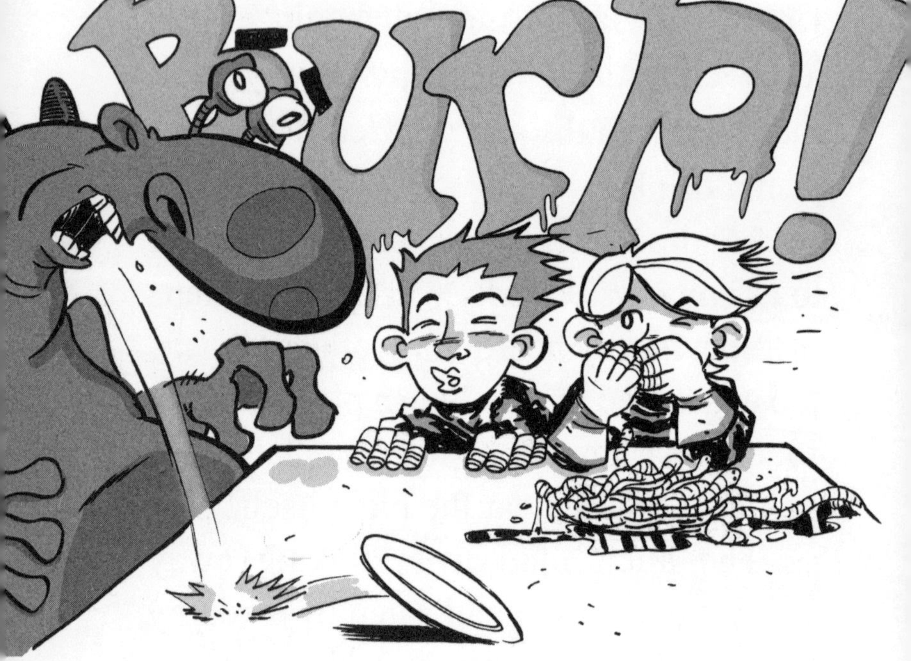
BURP!

"That's funny coming from the king of smells, himself!" Stan teased.

After a while of playing capture-your-food, Stinky and Stan were treated to some unusual musical entertainment.

Five Uranusings lined up in a row in front of what looked like a very long keyboard. Then, instead of using their hands to play the keys, they used their eyeballs!

Stan nudged his brother. "I'm not sure what's worse: watching them hurt themselves or the actual music."

Stan had a point. The music was pretty painful to human ears. It sounded like a bunch of cats having a hairball contest. The concert went on and on. When it was finally finished, Stan and Stinky clapped the loudest—mostly because it was over!

Stan used the Transalienator to ask the musicians why they don't just use their hands to play the music.

"Hands? How ridiculous!" the Uranusings responded.

Stinky and Stan just smiled at each other and shook their heads.

"This sure isn't Burbsburg," Stan said.

## CHAPTER SIX

## STINKY'S STINK

The next day, Stinky and Stan were awakened early and taken out to the blue, rolling fields of Uranus. When they arrived, they saw a familiar sight . . .

"Look!" cried Stinky. "It's our rocket!"

The boys ran over to check it out.

"P.U.!" Stan cried. "What stinks?"

"Hey, it's not me," said Stinky. "For once," he added with a grin.

"It must be the fart fuel from the rocket," said Stan. "I can't believe it's lasted this long."

This made the boys strangely proud.

Just then, Nerk and Fring came over. Fring explained that this was the place where they tried to grow Uranusing vegetables: *gax, durbrouts, chichigriz,* and the very popular *crollyshnots.*

"You know, no matter what planet we're on, I still don't like vegetables," Stan whispered to his brother.

News about Stinky and Stan's abilities had spread quickly, so tons of Uranusings had come to watch. They pushed and shoved each other, trying to get a good view. The crowd swelled, and soon there were big butts as far as the eye could see.

Finally, it was time for Stinky and Stan to show what they could do.

And what a show it was . . .

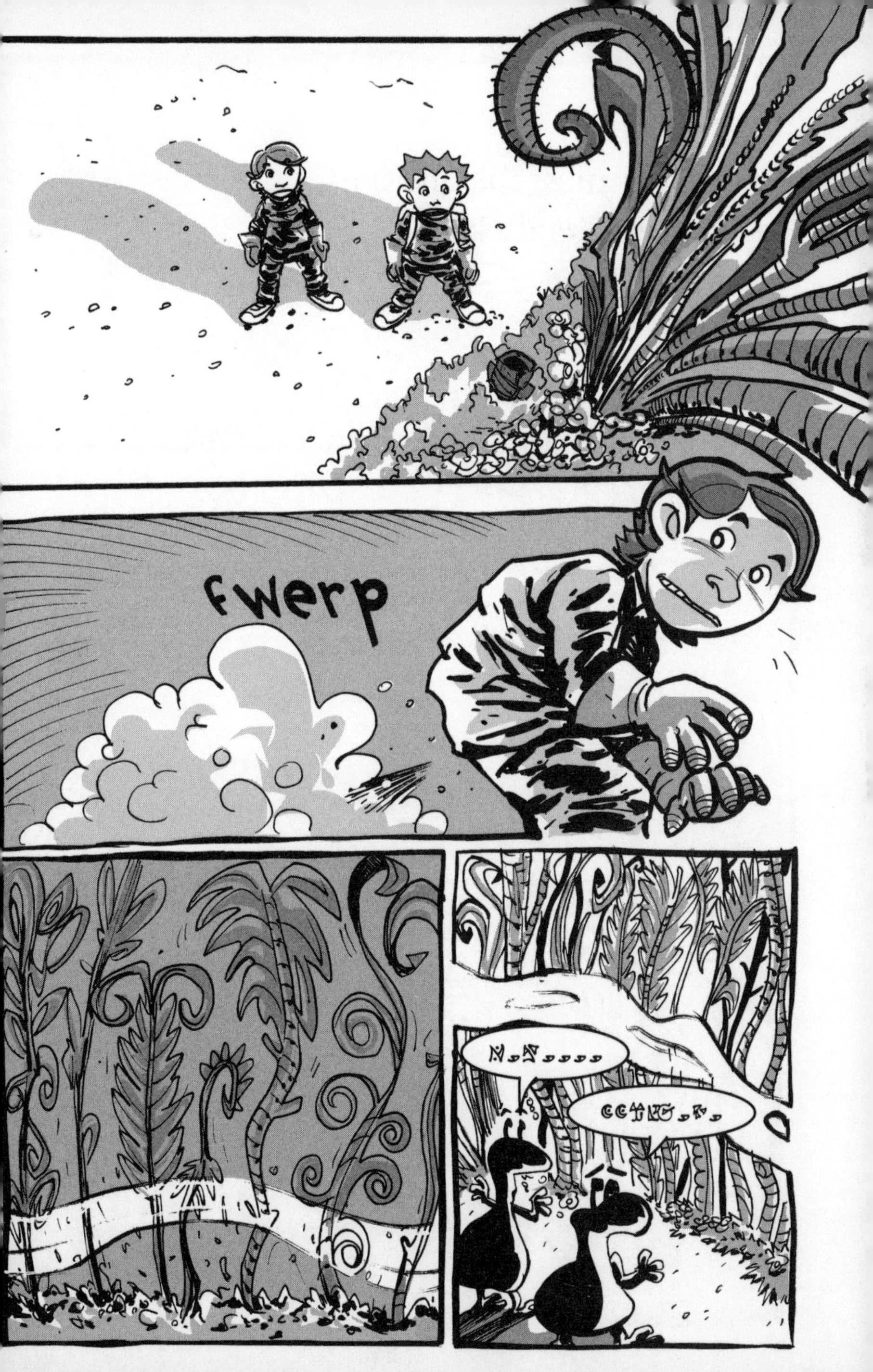
fwerp

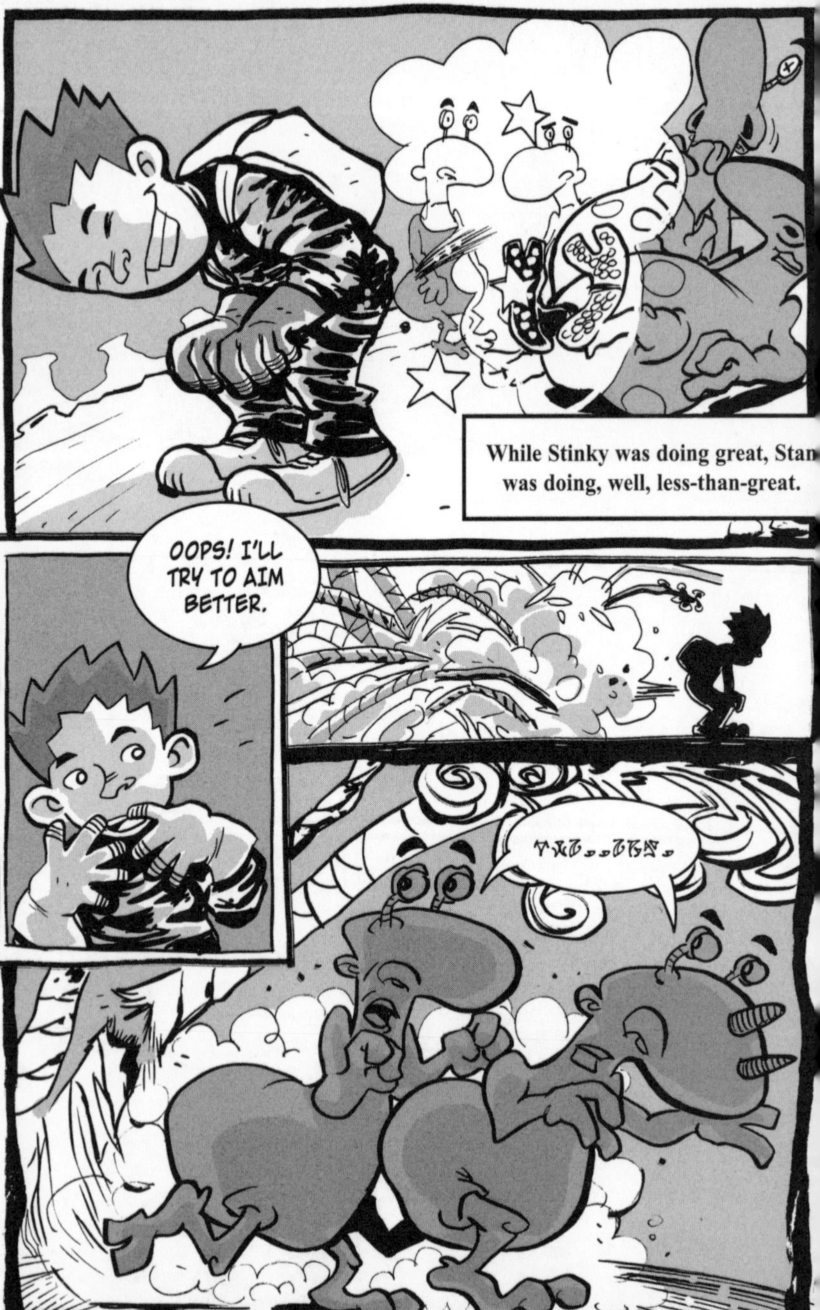
While Stinky was doing great, Stan was doing, well, less-than-great.
OOPS! I'LL TRY TO AIM BETTER.

Once the show was over, and all the Uranusings secured a safe spot away from the falling vegetation, Stan felt the need to apologize.

"Sorry!" he called, slightly embarrassed. Stan looked over at his brother, who was surrounded by Uranusings. They were clapping and cheering. Stinky was beaming.

"It must be the smell," Stan said to himself, feeling slightly bitter.

Judging from the damage he had done, Stan thought it might be better to take a little break from his own farting. He sat down and watched Stinky.

The more Stinky caused vegetables to grow, the more the Uranusings celebrated him. Soon, Stan was beginning to regret that he had pressured Stinky into coming to Uranus.

Feeling bored and left out, Stan decided to leave and go exploring.

"No one will miss me anyway," he muttered under his breath.

Stan walked away from the fields. A little while later, a smile spread across his face. Up ahead he saw the Gas Geysers.

"Cool!" Stan said excitedly.

He made his way to the entrance of the Gas Geysers. He ran up and got in line.

Stan watched what the Uranusings did, and soon it was his turn. He went over to an available geyser and . . .

*WHOOSH!*

He was shot up into the air.

"Whoa!" exclaimed Stan.

But there was one thing he hadn't thought about . . . coming back down! He didn't have a big butt like the Uranusings to soften the landing. Yes indeed, Stan was arriving without any landing gear!

Stan began to panic. The ground below was getting closer and closer . . . and then he farted!

Suddenly he was propelled back up into the air.

"Whew!" Stan sighed in relief. "I love when farting comes in handy, or saves my life!"

With a few more strategic farts, Stan landed safely on the ground, quite a distance from where he started.

*That might be enough exploring for one afternoon,* he thought, glad to be back on solid ground again. "I'd better head back," he said.

Stan looked around to find someone he could ask for directions. He didn't have to look long. An older-looking Uranusing approached him, holding a newspaper in his hand.

"⚒🝙⚐⚹🝚⚒🝞," said the Uranusing, pointing to the newspaper. A picture of Stinky and Stan was plastered on the front page.

Word must have spread super-fast around Uranus to have made front-page news, which was usually reserved for intergalactic battles and spelling bee results. Yes, it had been confirmed:

*Heroes of Uranus

Stinky and Stan were the hottest thing on Uranus since the Giant Plixie Sploot of '02.

Using the Transalienator, Stan asked the Uranusing, "Can you tell me how to get to the palace?"

*"Fuzzlenut,"* spit out the translating device.

*"Fuzzlenut?"* Stan asked, puzzled. "Hmm . . . maybe the Transalienator is acting up again." He pushed a button and seemed to get a better answer from the Uranusing: "Yes, of course. You go along this road for about seven *wigglewatts* and then turn left at the sign marked *Snugchump.*"

"Thank you," Stan translated back.

Although he wasn't sure what a *wigglewatt* was, at least Stan was pointed in the right direction.

## CHAPTER SEVEN

### TROUBLE ON URANUS

Meanwhile, Stinky had transformed a once-empty field into a colorful garden filled with blooms of every variety. Stinky felt like it was time for a break. Farting, although quite natural for Stinky, did take some effort. Besides, he loved it when the Uranusings pampered him—which happened pretty much all the time.

While Stinky relaxed on his lounge chair, he could hear Nerk and Fring jabbering something to him in alien speak. But Stinky couldn't understand a word they were saying.

*Where's the Transalienator?* he thought. Then, for the first time in a while, he wondered where Stan was. He had been enjoying all the attention so much that he hadn't noticed that Stan wasn't there.

"Maybe he's farting on his own patch of land somewhere else," he told himself. "Anyway, what do I need the Transalienator for? They love me here!" So he got back to enjoying himself.

"If only it was like this back on Earth," Stinky daydreamed. He was thrilled to finally be in a place where he and his farting were appreciated.

"I could stay here forever!" he said with a happy sigh.

Little did he know that was just what the Uranusings had in mind . . .

While Stinky had been busy being waited on and tended to, Stan made his way back to the palace. He had begun to look for Stinky when he heard voices up ahead. Stan darted behind a giant *crollyshnot* stalk and listened with the help of the Transalienator . . .

*The plan is going better than expected. I have never seen the fields so bountiful.

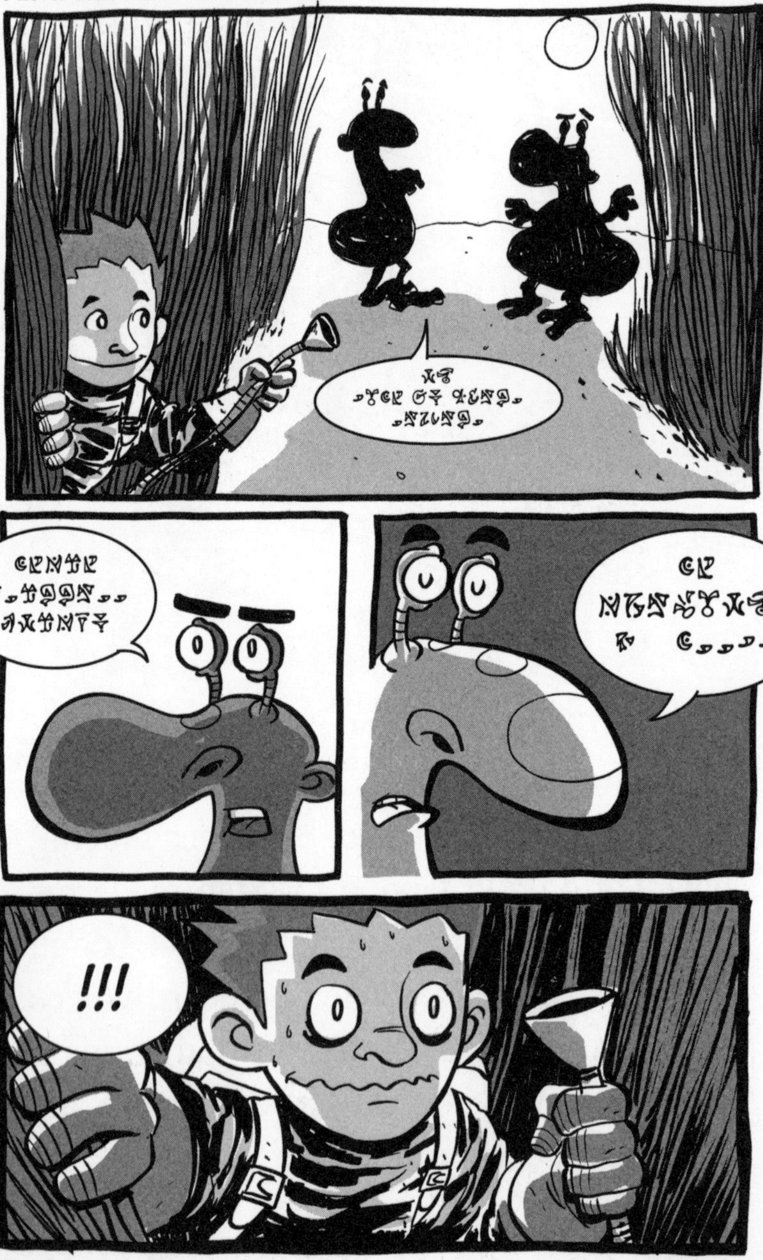
!!!

*There is no way we can let the boys go back to Earth now. They are too important to us here.

*Stinky is important. Stan I could do without.

*But we must be careful how we handle this . . .

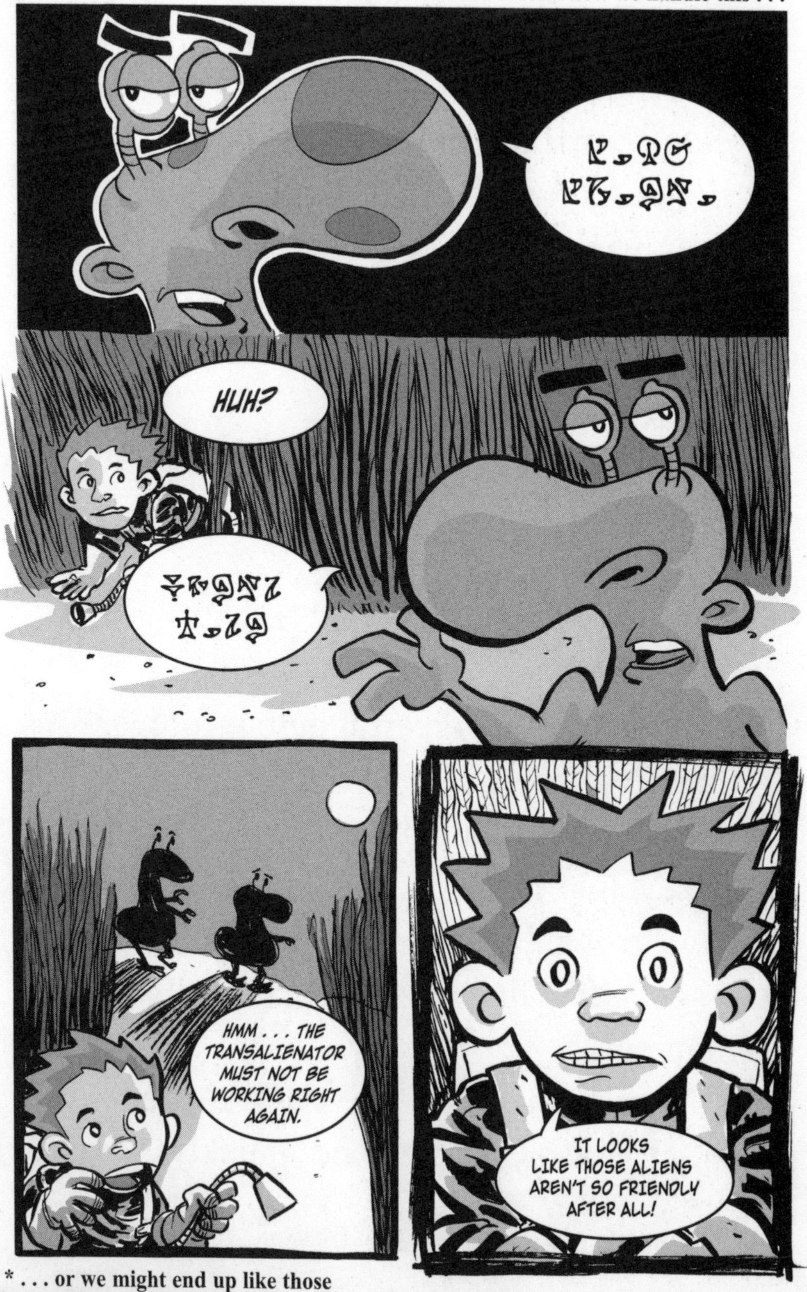
HUH?
HMM . . . THE TRANSALIENATOR MUST NOT BE WORKING RIGHT AGAIN.
IT LOOKS LIKE THOSE ALIENS AREN'T SO FRIENDLY AFTER ALL!

* . . . or we might end up like those frozen aliens they had in their room!

After overhearing the aliens' scheme, Stan constantly tried to get Stinky alone so he could tell him about the Uranusings' plan. But Stinky was never alone. That was, until after the big evening feast. Finally, the brothers were all by themselves.

"Stinky, I have to talk to you," Stan began. "The Uranusings are not who they seem to be."

Stinky looked at him. "Huh? What do you mean?"

"They want to keep us here—forever!" Stan explained.

"Don't be ridiculous," replied Stinky. "They just need us until all their crops have grown."

"And what about next season?" Stan said.

Stinky paused. He hadn't thought about that. But then he quickly said,

"What if they do want to keep us here? So what?"

"So what?!" exclaimed Stan.

"Yeah, so what?" said Stinky. "We get treated better here than at home."

"*You* get treated better," Stan pointed out. "I'm of no use to them. My farts don't smell; they just knock things over."

"Well, they *love* me here," said Stinky, defiantly. "Why would *I* want to leave?"

"They don't love you; they love your farts," said Stan, becoming frustrated.

"What's the difference?" Stinky asked even though he sort of already knew the answer.

"The difference is that we are Earthlings. We belong on *Earth,*" replied Stan. "This has been a great adventure, but come on, Stinky, we've got to go home."

But Stinky wasn't about to give up the royal treatment he'd grown used to.

"I'm not going anywhere," Stinky said and folded his arms. "If you don't like it here, then why don't you just go?"

"Without you?" Stan asked.

"Yeah!" Stinky said.

"Oh, sure," said Stan. "And how would I explain that one to Mom? 'I'm sorry, but Stinky has decided to stay on Uranus'?!"

But Stinky wouldn't budge. And for the first time, saying "Uranus" didn't make either one of them laugh.

## CHAPTER EIGHT

## IT BEGAN WITH A PIZZA

Over the next few weeks, Stinky and Stan saw very little of each other. Stinky continued to be treated like royalty, while Stan continued to just get the royal brush-off. Even when they *were* together, the brothers didn't have much to say to each other.

Then one evening, Stinky looked down at his plate of food and realized that there was no way he could face another creepy-crawly meal. What he really, really, really wanted was . . . pizza!

Suddenly, Stinky started to think about all the other things he missed on Earth: ice cream, books, TV on the weekends. But what he missed most of all was playing "explorers" with Stan. He missed his brother!

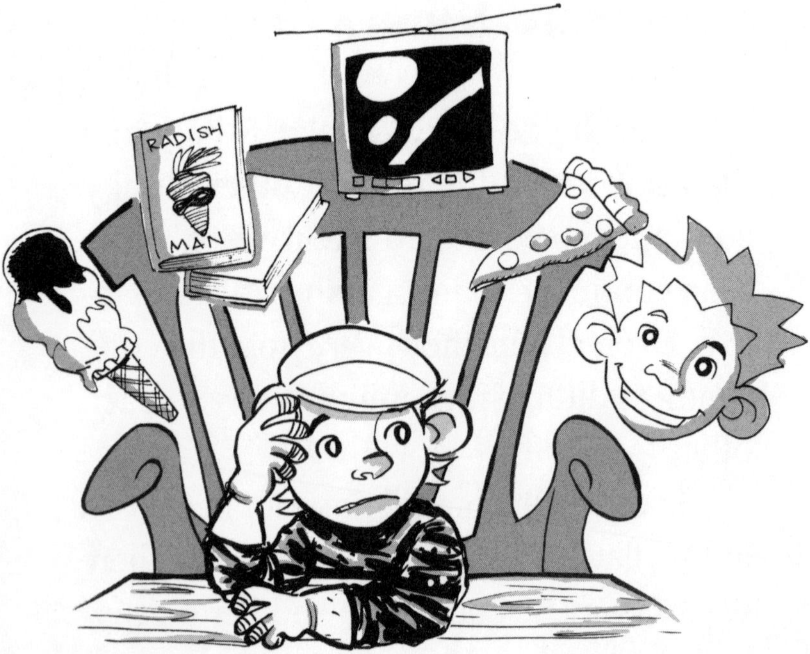
RADISH
MAN

Stinky looked around, but Stan wasn't there. He didn't bother going to the feasts anymore. So Stinky went to search for him.

He finally found him by the Gas Geysers.

"Stan!" called Stinky.

Stan spun around. "What are you doing here? Shouldn't you be getting fed grapes or doing something *royal?*" he said bitterly.

"All right, I probably deserve that," Stinky said. "Look, I'm sorry. I'm sorry about everything. I was being a jerk."

Stan was surprised and pleased that Stinky was back to his normal self.

"Aw, don't worry about it," said Stan. "I can see how the 'being-treated-like-a-king' thing would be appealing."

"For a while," said Stinky. "But it's more fun when you're around. Let's just go home."

Stan couldn't believe what he was hearing. "Really? You mean it?"

"Yup," answered Stinky.

"Cool!" exclaimed Stan. "But wait . . . the Uranusings are never going to let you leave."

"I know," agreed Stinky. "So I have a foolproof plan."

Stan grinned. "I like the sound of that!"

## CHAPTER NINE

## ROYAL AND NOT-SO-LOYAL

The next morning, the plan went into action. Stinky and Stan had gathered Nerk, Fring, and the rest of the Uranusings at the Spaceport.

Using the Transalienator, Stinky told them that he couldn't fart any longer.

"We are sad to go," Stinky said. "But I'm afraid we are no longer of use to you."

Then, on Stan's suggestion, Stinky

showed them. He walked over to a nearby patch of land and tried to fart, but nothing happened.

The Uranusings gasped. How could this happen?

"What will we do without Stinky?" worried Nerk. "How will our vegetables grow?"

The Uranusings whispered to each other nervously.

Stinky cleared his throat, and in his most powerful-sounding voice, he requested a spaceship to take him and Stan back to Earth.

Through the Transalienator, the Uranusings said they would get a spaceship and a pilot right away. They bowed and expressed their extreme disappointment at Stinky's departure.

Within a few minutes, a spaceship flew into view . . . and backfired.

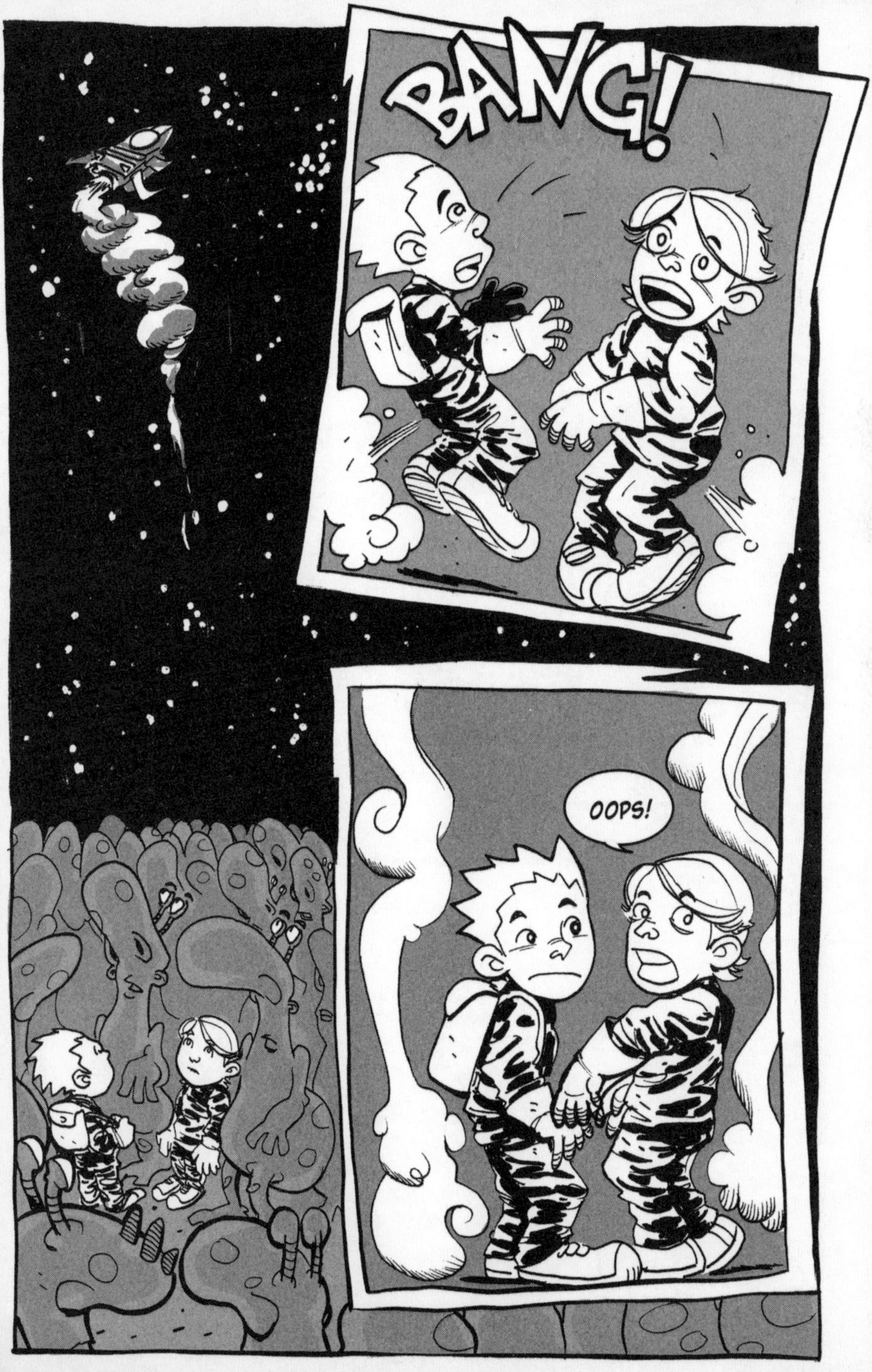
BANG!
OOPS!

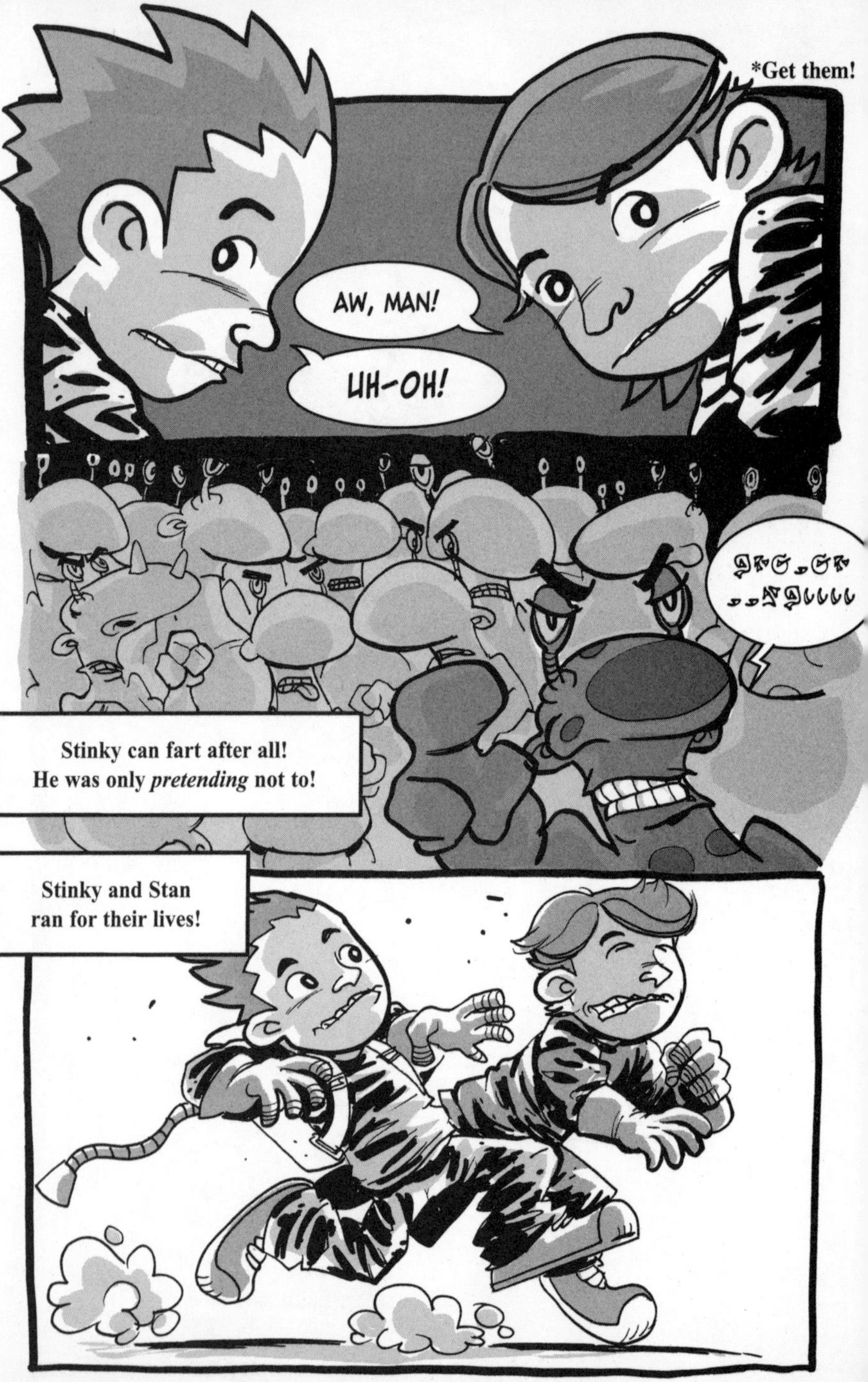
AW, MAN!
UH-OH!
*Get them!
Stinky can fart after all! He was only *pretending* not to!
Stinky and Stan ran for their lives!

The boys just kept on running. They headed toward the Gas Geysers.

"Use your farts to help you come down," Stan told Stinky.

"How do you know that?" Stinky yelled.

"Let's say that I've had a lot of time on my hands lately!" Stan yelled back.

They each bounced from one geyser to another and farted their way around Uranus.

"Head for the fields!" Stinky called as he shot up from a gas geyser.

Stan followed behind.

And so did the Uranusings!

The boys bounced into the fields and then tumbled to the ground.

"Are you all right?" Stinky asked Stan.

"Except for the crazy Uranusings following us, I'm just great," answered Stan.

Stinky and Stan ducked behind some extremely large *crollyshnots*.

"Good job on the vegetable growing, Stink," Stan whispered.

Stinky smiled at his brother. "Thanks. Who knew they would come in handy as a hideout?!"

"Shhh!" Stan said suddenly.

Nerk and Fring were nearby, but they didn't see Stinky and Stan hiding. Very carefully, Stan pointed the Transalienator mouthpiece in their direction to translate what the Uranusings were saying. He kept the volume very low.

"Come on out, boys," Nerk called.

"You can't hide forever," added Fring.

But the Transalienator also picked up when Nerk whispered to Fring, "Be careful what you say, or they might freeze us!"

" 'Freeze us'?" whispered Stinky. "What does he mean by that?"

"I've heard them say that before," whispered Stan. "I thought that the Transalienator just wasn't working right."

"Well, whatever it means, it sounds like they are afraid of us," said Stinky. "And that's definitely a good thing."

The boys tried hard to figure out what the Uranusings meant by "frozen."

Stan thought back to when he overheard the Uranusings talking about something frozen they had seen in the boys' room. Then he remembered the Uranusings holding the action figures.

"I've got it!" Stan said suddenly. "The Uranusings think our alien action figures are *real* aliens that we somehow froze!"

"That's crazy!" said Stinky.

"I know," said Stan, "but it kind of

makes sense. It's not like they would know any differently."

Stinky thought a moment. "Hmm . . . I think you're right," he finally said. Then he added, "Man, what I wouldn't give for a Uranusing action figure right now. Just to scare them with!"

Stan's eyes lit up. He quickly searched through his backpack, hoping to find a forgotten alien action figure. Instead he found two unused pieces of gum, a pencil, a *Pasteman* comic book, and a Captain Ammo action figure.

"Great!" Stinky exclaimed, grabbing Captain Ammo.

"But he doesn't look much like a Uranusing," said Stan. "He doesn't even look like an alien."

"Not yet," said Stinky. Then he took the gum out of the wrappers and put it in his mouth.

Stan was puzzled. "We're in danger here, and you're chewing gum?"

"Just wait," said Stinky.

Then he grabbed the gum wrappers and rolled up each piece. Next he took the gum out of his mouth and stuck a piece of it on each end of the rolled-up gum wrappers. Soon, there were two eyestalks—just like the Uranusings!

With another piece of chewed-up gum and some dirt, Stinky gave the figure a large nose and butt.

Stan patted his brother on the back. "Hey Stink, good work!"

But would the plan work on the Uranusings . . . ?

## CHAPTER TEN

## A VERY GROSSE ESCAPE

Stinky handed the "frozen" Uranusing to Stan. "Ready?" he asked.

"Yeah!" said Stan. "Let's go kick some Uranusing butt!"

Stinky grinned. "Or at least scare them into thinking we can!"

The boys ran out from their hiding place and toward the Spaceport. As expected, the Uranusings followed.

Finally, the boys made it to the port.

"Look!" said Stinky. "There's a spaceship!"

They ran over to it, and Stinky got in. But before Stan got in, he grabbed the Transalienator and turned to face the Uranusings.

"If you follow us," said Stan, "you will leave us with no choice, and THIS will happen to you!"

Stan held up the fake Uranusing figure.

"⚔︎♋︎♐︎♓︎♒︎⚒︎♈︎♐︎♌︎♐︎♊︎♐︎♋︎♊︎♐︎♒︎♑︎ ♊︎♐︎♓︎♒︎♒︎!" cried the Uranusings. They ran off, terrified.

Stinky and Stan's plan had worked!

Stan hopped into the spaceship and buckled up. He looked at Stinky in the pilot seat and said, "You don't know how to fly a spaceship!"

Stinky shrugged. "It's just like a videogame, right?"

Well, not quite . . .

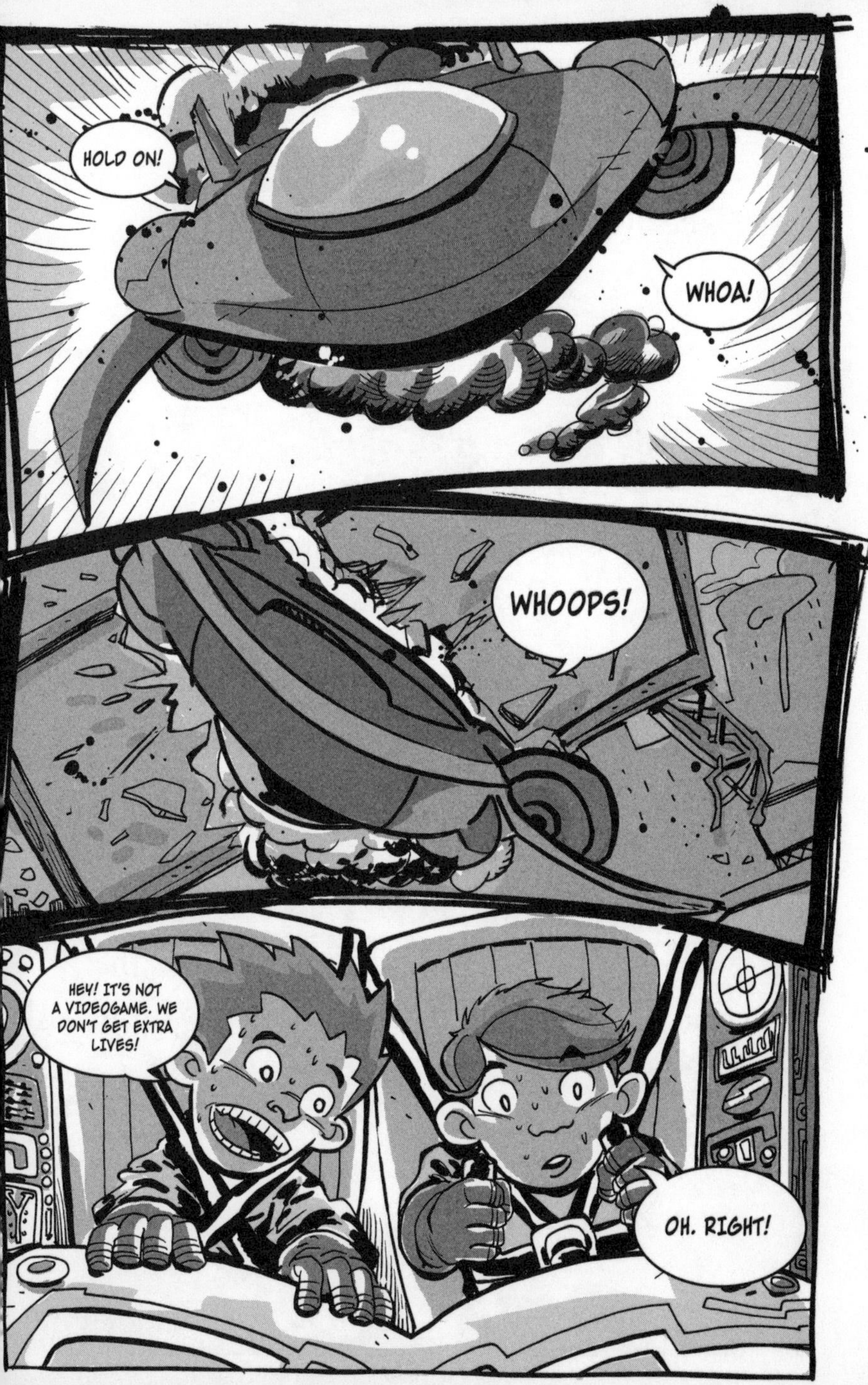
HOLD ON!
WHOA!
WHOOPS!
HEY! IT'S NOT A VIDEOGAME. WE DON'T GET EXTRA LIVES!
OH. RIGHT!

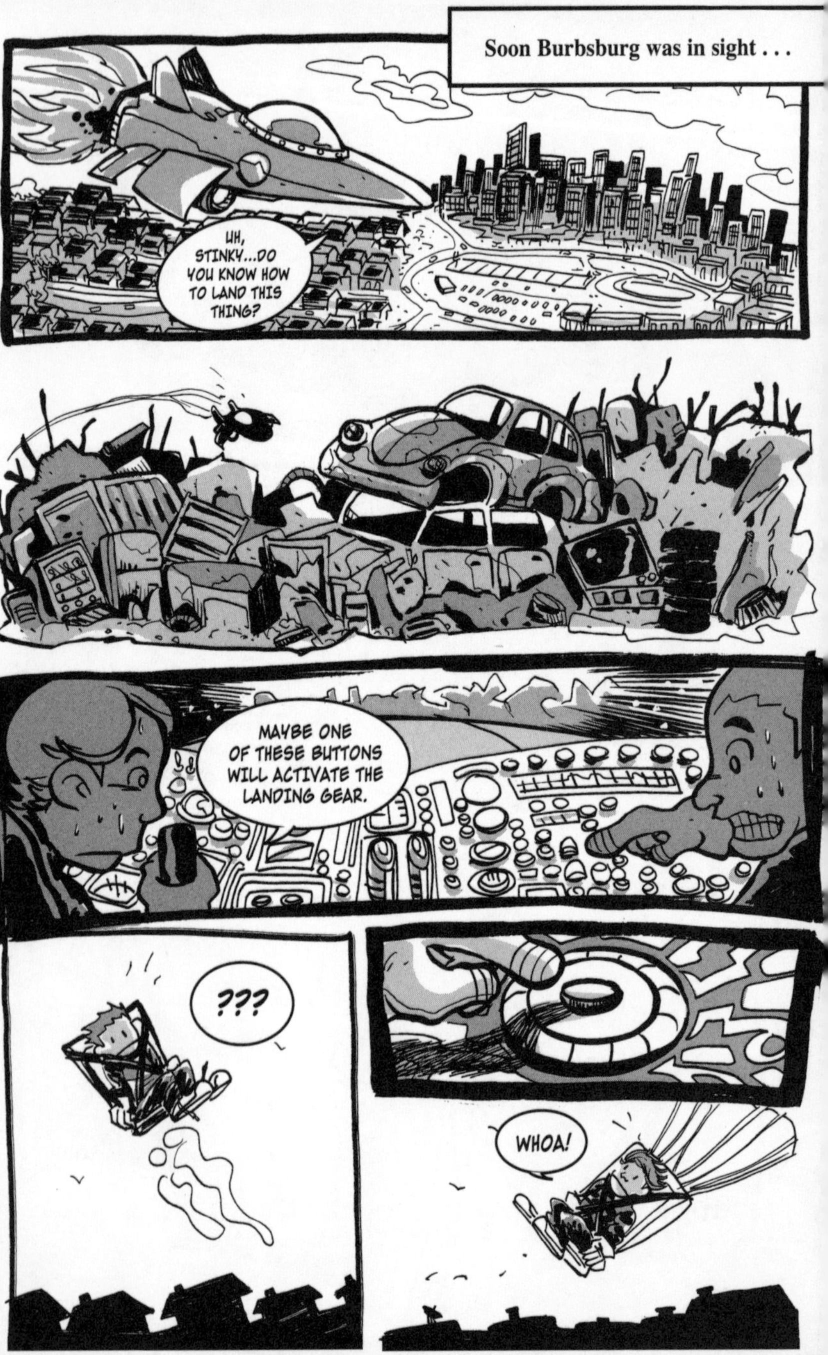
Soon Burbsburg was in sight . . .
UH, STINKY...DO YOU KNOW HOW TO LAND THIS THING?
MAYBE ONE OF THESE BUTTONS WILL ACTIVATE THE LANDING GEAR.
???
WHOA!

The boys landed roughly on the ground. They were bruised, but safe.

"I never thought I'd be so excited to be back in Burbsburg!" said Stan.

"You said it," Stinky agreed.

"We'd better get home," said Stan.

"On the way," said Stinky, "we'd better think of what to tell Mom."

"Oh, no!" said Stan. "You're right."

But at home, the boys were in for a surprise. Time had stood still since they left, and Eugene was *still* lying on their bedroom floor.

"Eugene! Eugene!" the boys called to him.

Eugene stirred a bit and then came to.

"What happened?" he asked.

Stan laughed. "What *didn't* happen!"

Then the brothers told Eugene all about their adventures on Uranus.

Eugene was pretty disappointed that he had fainted, but the fact that his Transalienator had worked seemed to cheer him up.

That night, before they went to bed, Stinky and Stan talked about what had happened.

"No one will believe us," Stinky said.

"It'll just have to be our secret," said Stan.

"You know," said Stinky, "if I never see another alien again, that'd be fine with me."

"I'm right there with you, bro," said Stan. "Maybe we'll just have to be admired on *this* planet instead."

"It sure is good to be home," said Stan.

Just then, they heard Patty yelling down the hall.

"Well, almost," Stinky added with a laugh.

Then the boys went to sleep, exhausted from their out-of-this-world adventure.